LAND OF SUN AND FLOWERS

Books by Voncille Shipley

Land of Sun and Flowers
This Raw, Red Land

LAND OF SUN AND FLOWERS

Sequel to This Raw, Red Land

Voncille Shipley

For Voncille & Jack

Sunny Days

Voncille Shipley

29 May 2004

iUniverse, Inc.

New York Lincoln Shanghai

Land of Sun and Flowers
Sequel to This Raw, Red Land

iUniverse, Inc.

For information address:
iUniverse, Inc.
2021 Pine Lake Road, Suite 100
Lincoln, NE 68512
www.iuniverse.com

This book is a work of fiction. All names, characters, and incidents are either the product of the author's imagination or are used fictitiously. All town names used are of actual places but are used fictitiously. Chagris had a post office from 1896 to 1909 but any other depiction of this town is fictitious.

ISBN: 0-595-30705-1

Printed in the United States of America

As always, for my husband, John,
and for my brother, Glynn Emberling

OKLAHOMA A TOAST

By HARRIETT PARKER CAMDEN
(Used by permission of the copyright owners,
Chenoweth & Green, Enid, Oklahoma)

I give you a land of sun and flow'rs,
And summer a whole year long;
I give you a land where the golden hours
Roll by to the mocking bird's song;
Where the cotton blooms 'neath the southern sun,
Where the vintage hangs thick on the vine;
A land whose story has just begun,
This wonderful land of mine.

CHORUS

Oklahoma, Oklahoma;
Fairest daughter of the West;
Oklahoma, Oklahoma,
'Tis the land I love the best.
We have often sung her praises,
But we have not told the half,
So I give you "Ok-la-ho-ma,"
'Tis a toast we all can quaff.

A land where the fields of golden grain,
Like waves on a sunlit sea,
Bend low in the breezes that sweep the plain
With a welcome to you and me;

Where the corn grows high 'neath the smiling sky,
Where the quail whistles low in the grass;
And the fruit trees greet with a burden sweet,
And perfume the winds that pass.
                              Chorus

Prologue

The heavy jeans quilt that Lillie had brought along on their trip felt good tucked across their laps and wrapped around their legs and feet. He had chuckled as she packed so many clothes for such a short trip but she had reminded him that you never could tell what kind of weather to look for in Oklahoma this time of year. Now he relished the warmth of his old sheepskin-lined coat as the north wind whistled around the flaps of the buggy.

"Are you warm enough, Lillie?" he asked.

"Yes, Matt, I have this wool shawl pulled tight around my coat. It feels pretty good." She smiled at him, her old happy smile from days gone by.

"Maybe it will warm up when the sun gets a little higher. This black buggy will hold the heat."

While he got up courage to talk about the four children who had caused them so much grief, he filled the time with inconsequential chatter. He didn't know how to start but he had made her a promise and putting it off wouldn't make it any easier. Lillie seemed to be waiting calmly for him to speak but he knew her too well. She felt uneasy inside and anxious to have everything out in the open, as she had said.

He stopped talking and stared at the horse's rump. Maybe he'd better get his facts lined up before she asked any questions. His Texas Ranger training stood him in good stead. She knew almost as much about Paul's ambush and murder as he did. He never had told her how Paul begged him to tell him what to do about turning in Buford and the Sexton boys for horse stealing—the same theft for which the Sexton brothers had been bound over for trial yesterday in District Court in Ardmore. Her emotions were too raw to bear much more because they had failed to bind the two men for trial in Paul's murder. An open-and-shut case in his opinion, the authorities nevertheless found no witnesses and little circumstantial evidence.

Talking about Buford would be easier. After Paul's ambush he had pinned Buford down and made him admit his association with the Sextons. His big mistake had been in not keeping an eye on Buford allowing him to skip the country that night rather than face the authorities. Lillie knew most of it. She had talked about watching Buford and her brother-in-law's dog leave a couple of hours before daylight. In a roundabout way they had heard of Buford because Lillie's sister Betty wrote that they found the dog at their home in Texas a few days later. The authorities hadn't found Buford yet but he fully expected that they soon would bring him back for trial.

His thoughts shifted to Flora's elopement the night after Paul's funeral. Ida had conspired to help her slip away and be gone too far for him to stop the marriage. Her complicity didn't surprise him; a romantic fifteen-year-old thought it high adventure. But seventeen-year-old Flora had never before defied him. She had run off and married an Indian after he had expressly forbid it. She tried to convince him her Plez was gentle and better educated than she but at the time he could still hear the savage yell as he watched a Comanche kill his brother Paul back in Texas in the uprising of seventy-three. Time and circumstance had convinced him to ask his son-in-law's forgiveness and he intended to take care of that as soon as they got home.

He felt such a failure with those three but his being an accomplice in Jed's fiasco broke his heart. At nineteen Jed remained such a kid in so many ways. Carefree and happily in love with Esther McMasters, he had messed up his life by dallying with Vinnie Wade.

Abruptly, he said, "Which one do you want to talk about first?"

She didn't hesitate. "Jed. I want to know all about what happened the day he got married. I have so many questions. Tell me everything."

Where to start? "You know Jed and Ben and I were harvesting corn that day. You and the girls had gone to that quilting bee and Holt was in school. Well, along about dinnertime, Hiram Wade rode up on his horse and reined him right in front of Jed. Then he pulled his shotgun out of the saddle holster and laid it across in front of him. I could see how serious this affair might turn out, so I walked over and invited Wade to state his business."

Matt looked at Lillie and saw tension in every line of her body. I don't know whether she needs to know all the conversation or not, he thought. I'll clean it up for her at the very least.

"Wade didn't waste any words. He said, 'I come after your son here to marry my daughter.' I was afraid to take my eyes from him because he sounded so mean, so I asked Jed, 'What do you know about this?'

"Jed didn't deny it. In fact, he didn't say a word but I glanced over at him and I could see guilt written all over his face. Wade let out an oath. I've heard some as bad in my day but none worse. He told us that no matter what Jed said about it there *would* to be a wedding that day.

"I told him that at Jed's age he couldn't marry without my approval. I found him a hard man to deal with but I finally convinced him to meet us in town at the deputy clerk's house. I gave him my word that I would bring Jed and he agreed to go home and get his daughter."

Tears ran down Lillie's cheeks unchecked. In a choked voice, she said, "So he believed you and went home?"

"I told you I gave him my word."

"What did Jed do?"

"He cried and begged me not to make him marry that girl. Lillie, that just tore my heart out. I asked him if the child could be his."

"What did he say?"

"You didn't know it, but I had asked him once before. I knew he had something on his mind and, when I heard about the girl appearing at the dance and them leaving together, I suspicioned this very thing. But he denied it then. So I asked him again and he admitted the possibility."

"Possibility? Is that enough to ruin his life over?"

"That's been eating at me ever since. But I didn't see what else I could do. I had given Wade my word because he might have shot Jed. I just didn't know for sure that he wouldn't. He's high tempered; I could tell. So I told Jed to get dressed for his wedding and I went in and put on my good clothes."

Lillie swiped at her face with a gloved hand. Matt pulled his handkerchief from his pocket and handed it to her. "He left a note for Esther," she said.

"Yes, he asked me to let him at least do that. Lillie, I've never felt so sorry for anyone in my life. He knew we didn't want the girl here, so he packed his clothes and took his gun and his horse." Matt strangled on the last words. Lillie put her arms around him and laid her head on his shoulder. They cried together while the horse plodded on.

SPRING 1908

CHAPTER 1

Lillie

Lillie Conover laid a butcher knife in the big dishpan and paused to take a quick look around the room before she went to gather leaf lettuce, radishes, and green onions for the wilted salad she planned for the noon meal. A big pot of dried black-eyed peas simmered on the back of the range and the last few sweet potatoes waited buttered and ready to bake in a large bread pan. She would put them in the oven while she stirred up the cornbread and finish baking them together.

Warm Spring sunshine greeted her as she stepped out the back door and, exhilarated, she drank in a deep breath of the fresh air. She turned her back to the sun and stood looking at the expanse of plowed red earth, watching her brood as they stooped, dropped seeds and covered them, straightened and tamped the earth with a foot before moving to the next drop. All her family, even little Betsy, had gone to the field right after breakfast to plant cotton.

She turned completely around surveying her domain. Beyond the cotton fields dark green covered the earth where field corn had emerged already. When they completed planting both upland and bottom land fields with cotton, they would move to that area to hoe corn. She wondered if any woman in the world felt more blessed this morning than she.

She considered checking to see if she needed to corral Betsy but decided to let Matt send her to the house when if she got in his way. If anything, he indulged the child more than she did. However, Betsy had become a good little worker ever since they had helped Ben gather his pecans over the fall and winter. He had let her pick up on the halves and she loved getting money of her own when he sold the pecans.

As Lillie rounded the corner of the house headed for the kitchen garden, she saw Matt and Jed coming toward her. Surprised to see Jed in midmorning during planting season, she set the dishpan on a stump and went to meet them. Jed's worried expression alarmed her. Quickly counting Vinnie's due date, she feared the baby had come early.

Matt took her arm and turned her around to walk with them. "Jed has a problem he needs to talk over with us," he said. "He's afraid to worry you but I told him that you are perfectly well now and he can tell us plainly just what the situation is. I told Ben to keep the other children in the field until we called them."

The explanation did little to alleviate her apprehension. She said to Jed, "Is Vinnie all right?"

"Now, Lillie, wait till we get in the house and let Jed tell it his own way," Matt said.

Once in the kitchen, Matt sat at the table and pulled out a chair for her. She expected Jed to sit across the table from them but he paced back and forth, too agitated to sit.

Lillie repeated her question.

"I guess she is, Ma. At least she says she is. But I had to get her out of that house and away from her Pa. We can't go back. I don't know what to do."

Matt rose from his chair, went to Jed and put his arm around his shoulders. "Son, you've got to get hold of yourself. Come, sit down and tell your Ma and me all about it. Start from the beginning. What happened that you had to get Vinnie away?"

"Her Pa hit her; I'm afraid he hurt the baby." Jed wrenched away from his father's protective arm and stomped to the window. He stood looking out as if he could see a stage with performing actors.

A scene replayed in Lillie's mind at the words 'hurt the baby' and she saw once again her own injured baby and remembered the long-term consequences that eventually resulted in Terence's death. She pushed back her chair and rushed to the side of this child of hers who felt the same fear and anguish. Putting her arms around him, she turned him toward her and soothed him, patting his back as if he were five years old.

"Come, sit and tell us all about it," she said.

He allowed her to lead him to a chair. She sat beside him while he told his story.

"It's planting time, you know. It takes all hands at the Wade place, but those good-for-nothings the other girls married take off when there's work to do. I work my head off because that's the way you raised me. And the girls all work from daylight to dark as fast as they can.

"But this morning Vinnie woke up sick. She's way along now and getting really big." He hesitated and Lillie realized his embarrassment about discussing these details with his mother. She patted his big, work-roughened hands that lay clasped on the table.

"That's a bad time in a pregnancy," she said. She had never said that word in front of any man but Matt before and she felt a hot flush cover her face and neck. I had to say it to get this boy to open up, she rationalized.

He accepted her encouragement and went on. "Her back was killing her from all the stooping to drop seeds. After that, you know, she had to rake and firm the ground. She ached all night from all that stooping and raking and, this morning, she had a hard time getting out of bed. I remembered a little bit about when you had Betsy and I thought it might be her time to have the baby. I told her to stay around the house today and not go to the field."

Jed's voice had become raspy as he told his story. Lillie fetched him a drink of water and he gulped it gratefully before he went on. "She was afraid to tell her Pa so I told her I'd tell him. But she thought he'd take it better if she told him herself. And, when she said she didn't feel like going to the field today, he slapped her. I stepped between them facing him. I said, 'Vinnie is too sick to work today.' He swelled up like a toad and his face got beet-red. He shoved me aside and, before I could get my footing, he had hit Vinnie with his fist. The blow knocked her a-winding and she fell against a corner of the table. She screamed and doubled over grabbing her swollen belly. It scared the life out of me, I can tell you."

Matt slammed his open hand against the table. Lillie had seen the gesture before when he wanted to handle a situation at once and had no control over it. "So what did you do?" he said.

"I helped Vinnie up and gave her Pa a look that said he'd better not interfere. Then I guided her to our room, shut the door, and told her to lie down. But she said she wasn't hurt as bad as she thought at first. So I started grabbing our things and stuffing them in pillowcases. I told her we were getting out of there and not going back. She looked relieved, dumped the things out on the bed and began folding them and packing them. You may not know how neat she is, but everything has to be just so."

He paused and looked from one to the other of his parents. Neither of them said anything and he went on, "So I took my gun and went and saddled my horse. I didn't know what her Pa would try to do when we left, so I kept the gun at the ready when I went back in after her. But he didn't say a word. We loaded the sacks on the horse and I helped her mount. I walked because I didn't want to overload the horse."

Lillie waited for him to continue but he seemed to have finished his story. "Where is Vinnie now?" she asked.

"I didn't know where we would be welcome, so I took her to the one person I knew wouldn't turn us down—Sister Goodgion. And I came home."

Lillie looked at this distressed son and her heart ached for him. He's still a boy in so many ways, she thought, not yet twenty. Tears streaming down her face, she turned to face Matt and saw moisture in his eyes, too. He raised his eyebrows and she nodded.

"Come on, Jed. We'll hitch up the buggy and go get her," he said.

Two days later, Lillie grabbed a big dishpan and butcher knife, said, "I'll be back," and hurried out the door. If I had to spend another minute in the room with that woman, she thought, I'd have one of my spells.

Stopping by the cotton field, she called out, "I'm going to see if I can find some poke sallet."

"We're almost done here with the planting," Jed said. "I'll go help you."

Glad to have a little time alone with him, Lillie said, "Then let's see if we can get more than one mess and I'll can some. Get some tow sacks to carry it in."

"Ma, I saw a big patch in my pecan orchard," Ben called. "Try there."

Gulping a big breath of the fresh Spring air, Lillie filled her lungs to capacity and blew it out slowly. After repeating the process several times, she began to feel the tension in her neck and back ease. When Jed returned with the sacks, they covered the short distance to the pecan grove without talking. My happy boy has changed, Lillie thought. Time was when he would have chattered every step of the way.

During the winter, Ben had hacked out a lot of the undergrowth in the acreage he had bought from Plez's uncle. Piles of limbs dotted the grove waiting to be hauled away or burned. Jed's keen eyes soon spotted several patches of dark green plants and they approached the nearest one.

"Don't cut the big red stems," Lillie said. "Just get the tops of those. Ask me if you're not sure about any of them."

Jed favored her with a grin. "Ma, I'm an old married man. You don't think I know how to pick poke?"

That's better, Lillie thought. "I seem to remember you haven't had much experience at it," she said. "You pay attention to your old Ma and you'll learn how to do it right." She stooped and began to cut the greens and drop them in the dishpan.

His expression sobered. "Ma, I'm sorry we've had to impose on y'all like this. I didn't know what else to do."

She straightened to a standing position and rubbed her back. "Son, you know you can always come home when you need to. We'll get it all worked out, don't you worry."

Jed opened the long blade of his pocketknife and attacked the plants, slashing stems and wadding them by handfuls into one of the gunnysacks. "But I do worry. I have so much to worry about. Vinnie usually isn't this difficult to get along with. I'm sure she's worried that the baby is hurt. It's not like her to bottle anything up inside so I think she must be terrified. She thinks that if she says it outloud, it will come true. So she lashes out at everybody and everything."

"Jed, if anybody can sympathize with her, I can. That's probably what makes me so nervous. I remember so well when my own firstborn's injuries happened." She leaned over and massaged his tight neck with both hands. "We have to pray your baby will be all right."

His tears fell on the green leaves and he slowed the vicious strokes of his knife. Stuffing a mass of plants into his sack, he rocked back on his heels. "Ma, I've wondered all my life about what happened to my half-brother. He died before I was born and nobody ever talked about him to me until last fall. I asked Pa and he wouldn't go into detail. Now I may be facing the same heartache myself and I think it's time I heard the whole story."

Lillie's mind went back to that scene stamped so indelibly in her memory. She had tried to eradicate it, and time had dimmed it somewhat, but it returned in full force as she tried to find words to describe it to her son without embarrassing them both.

"Terence was five days old," she began. "I lived so far from my folks that none of them could come to help me. Karl's mother came to help out right after the baby's birth but he took her home that day leaving us alone until he got back. But he didn't come back right away. I had to get out of bed and fix me some supper and get clean didies for the baby. As it got later and later, I feared he had abandoned us."

Jed had quit gathering greens and sat on the warm ground. He shook out one of the sacks and spread it for her to sit on.

Pulling the dishpan to her, Lillie dumped the sack Jed had filled and began inspecting each plant, discarding damaged leaves and pulling off tough stems. "He came home way after dark," she continued. "I could tell he had been drinking the way he slammed the front door and stomped in with unsteady steps. Thankful that I hadn't lit a lamp, I hoped he'd leave the baby and me alone. I held Terence in my arms and listened, barely breathing.

"I heard him stumble around in the front room and then he threw the bedroom door open. He held a lamp in one hand and stumbled with each step. I just knew he'd set the house afire any minute. But he managed to set the lamp on the dresser and then he came and stood over the bed.

"'Put the baby down,' he said. 'I've been waiting long enough to take my wife back.'

"'It's too soon,' I told him. 'The baby is only five days old.'

"'The *baby*, the *baby*. All I hear out of you is how the baby keeps you from doing this or that. Well, this time, it's not going to work.'" She heard the exact tone of his voice again.

"I was petrified, let me tell you. He leaned right down over me and I couldn't escape. I hugged Terence closer and prayed for deliverance. But the old Devil himself indwelled him that night. With the lamp behind him, I couldn't see his face to read his expression and couldn't believe what happened next. He uttered an oath that I'd never heard before, tore Terence from my arms, and flung him across the room."

The vivid memory returned in all its horror. She saw again his long shadow hovering over her like a demon, felt the struggle for control of the baby, and heard the sickening thud of that tiny body hitting the floor. Mindless of the green and red stain from the poke sallet, she buried her face in her hands and sobbed.

Jed knelt beside her and cradled her while she cried. "Ma, you don't have to tell me any more if it hurts you so," he said.

Her sobs lessened until she stopped crying and dried her eyes. "No, I've got started now; I'll finish.

"I tried to get up and go to Terence, but Karl held me down. I fought him with everything in me, screaming at him that he had killed my baby. He *laughed*. I fought as long as I could but soon gave out being so weak from childbirth. That's when I heard Terence crying and realized that Karl hadn't killed him but knew he must have hurt him pretty bad.

"Karl didn't let me go until he no longer wanted me. I can still smell his whiskey breath and feel his scratchy whiskers. I can't abide either one to this day. When I got loose, I shot out of the bed and ran to Terence. He had screamed and cried at first but by that time he lay so still I picked him up and put my ear to his chest. His ragged breathing and faint heartbeat sent cold shivers all over me. I knew I had to get help for him.

"By this time, Karl snored in a stupor. I dressed as quickly as I could, wrapped Terence in a baby quilt Mama had mailed to me, and ran out of the house. I didn't know very many people there, but I did know where my mid-wife lived. I'll never forget my anxiety at starting out on that two-mile hike in the dark. After a while when my eyes got used to the darkness, I had no trouble staying in the road, though. I kept checking Terence's breathing and heartbeat and hurrying as fast as I could but still those were the longest miles I ever traveled."

She paused and took a long, unsteady breath. Looking at Jed for the first time since she had resumed her narrative, she saw that all the color had drained from his face. He's afraid for his own baby, she thought, and reached over and patted his hand. "Jed," she said, "nothing this bad has happened to Vinnie and the baby. The baby is still moving just like before and Vinnie is all right, too. Don't worry, Son, everything will work out, you'll see."

Jed tried to smile but didn't quite manage it. After a long silence, he said, "So what happened when you got to the midwife's?"

"She put us to bed and her husband brought the doctor. After he spent a long time examining Terence, he shook his head. He told me that the blow had hurt my baby inside, and if he lived, that he might never walk. He and the sheriff got in touch with my folks and they wired me a train ticket. I took my baby home. We had nothing but the clothes on our backs but those good people rounded up diapers for Terence and we made it just fine. Mama and my sisters and I nursed Terence night and day and little by little he gained strength. He did walk, later than most babies, but he was always sickly."

"I know about how Karl died; Pa told me. But did he give you any more trouble?"

"After about three weeks, he showed up at Pa's place and said he'd come after his family. My Pa met him on the front porch with his shotgun, pointed it at him and told him it had a hair trigger, and that it might go off if he ever set foot in that county again. I never heard from him directly again. I didn't know where he went or what he did until your Pa brought his death notice."

"He should have been hung."

"The sheriff did talk to him. He swore I dropped the baby—a feeble story but the sheriff told me it would be my word against his. I didn't push it. I never wanted to see him again. I wanted to be let alone with my baby to nurse him back to health. Jed, God has His own way of taking vengeance. Your Pa told me that Karl's horse kicked him to death, hurting him inside his body and in his head. That seemed just and fair to me. And for Terence and me, in a round-about way, his death sent us Matt."

Lillie got up and stuffed the picked-over poke in the sack she had been sitting on. "Let's finish here and get on back. I can clean these greens better at the house," she said.

CHAPTER 2

Lillie

That night, a scream wakened Lillie out of deep slumber. Before she could get her wits about her, she heard a long groan coming through the wall between her bedroom and that of Jed and Vinnie. It must be three o'clock in the morning, she thought as she stripped her gown over her head and slung it at the bed. Dressing quickly, she hurried to Vinnie's bedside. Vinnie lay panting and looked up at her with frightened eyes. Lillie touched the bed and found it wet.

Patting the woman's shoulder, she said, "It's all right, Vinnie. Your water broke."

Turning to her pale and shaken son, she said, "You need to go get a midwife. I haven't thought to ask around here. Do you know of one?"

"No," he said. "Vinnie, where can I get a midwife?"

"I don't know," she said. "We never used one at home. Ma took care of my sisters. She made each of them help her with the other one." Her speech ended in a moan as another contraction began.

Lillie stepped close to the bed. "Vinnie, try not to scream again. You'll wake the whole house and scare Betsy to death. Take my hands and hold on."

As Vinnie's grip tightened, Lillie turned to Jed. "Get your horse and go get Judith McMasters. I think we'll have plenty of time for her to get here." I don't know about that, she thought, but I need to get Jed out of here. And I do need her help. "Before you go, get that piece of roll of building paper we had left over from papering the front room and bring it in here. I'll spread it under Vinnie to protect the mattress."

Jed's white face turned a rosy red. "Ma, I can't do that," he said. "After what I did to Esther when I married Vinnie, I can't ask her Ma to come and help birth the baby."

Vinnie screamed again.

Lillie turned her attention back to the laboring girl. Vinnie lay back on the bed gasping for breath. Lillie patted her again. "Vinnie," she said. "I'm going with Jed into the next room to find the roll of paper for him. It'll be a while before your next pain and I'll be back before then."

Vinnie grasped her hand. "Don't leave me," she said. "Jed, don't leave me."

"Vinnie, you've got to get ahold of yourself," Lillie said. "This is no place for a man. Jed can't stay while the baby is being born. Let him do something useful."

She walked away from the bed. Motioning Jed to go with her, she said, "Come on, Jed. Let's go."

Jed followed her from the room leaving a weeping Vinnie behind. When his mother ducked behind the quilt covering a corner of the front room, he entered the dark space with her, whispering, "Ma, I mean it. I'd feel like a fool and a hypocrite asking Mrs. McMasters to lift a finger for me."

"It doesn't matter. I have to have help. Ida is too young and so is Polly Wilson. Besides, neither of them is married. Flora is married but we need another woman with experience. Judith is the only one within miles."

"What if she refuses to come?"

"She won't refuse, Jed. Any woman who has borne children will go help another when her time comes."

"But it's the middle of the night."

Exasperated, Lillie said, "Jed, quit arguing about it. I know it will be embarrassing for you as well as for them, but there is nothing else to be done."

He stood as if rooted to the spot.

Lillie rummaged in the quilt box until she felt the roll of paper. "Here, Jed, lift these quilts off of it while I pull out this roll," she said.

Following her directions, Jed lifted out a stack of quilts. She pulled the paper out and Jed dropped the quilts back in the box. I'll straighten them later, Lillie thought. "Now, go," she told Jed.

When they stepped out from behind the quilt, Ida greeted them from the bed that had been set in front of it. "What's going on?" she asked.

Oh, no, another complication, Lillie thought. I had hoped she would sleep through this. "The baby's on its way," she said to Ida. Then to Jed, "Son, be on your way."

She watched him out the door as she shushed Ida with a hand on her shoulder. Ida had started to rise but her mother pushed her back down. "Ida, the best way to help us is to see that Betsy doesn't get in the way if she wakes up. Jed is going after Mrs. McMasters."

Ida gasped. "How can you ask her to help out after the way that Jed and Vinnie treated Esther?"

"She's the only one available at this late date," Lillie said. "I feel sure she won't turn us down."

When she returned to the bedroom, she found an exhausted Vinnie lying on the bed with tears running down her temples and into her hair. "Have you had another pain?" Lillie asked.

"Yes," Vinnie said in a faint voice. "I bit my lip to keep from screaming."

Lillie patted her. "That's my brave girl," she said.

By the time Jed reappeared with Judith McMasters, Vinnie's contractions were coming closer together but Lillie judged that she had at least two more hours before the birth. She gestured to Judith to stop outside the room and went to her, pulling the door behind her until she could see Vinnie's bed through the crack.

Afraid anything she said might be taken the wrong way, she hesitated. Laying her hand on Judith's arm, she said, "Thank you for coming. I didn't know what else to do."

Judith smiled with closed lips. "I almost didn't. Everett answered the door and came back and got me. When I saw Jed at the door I came as close to fainting as I ever did in my life. You know how Everett is; he didn't say a word and the silence stretched on until Jed told me to my face what he wanted. He almost choked on the words. In a way I felt sorry for him.

"I said, 'Can you get a midwife?'

"Jed said, 'No time. I don't know where to find one, anyhow.'

"So I asked him, 'Why don't you get the girl's own mother?'

"He swallowed. I saw tears on his cheeks. 'She wouldn't come,' he said. 'We had such a row a couple of days ago we twisted off with her Pa. And her Ma won't cross him.'

"I knew then I couldn't turn him down. I'd go help any woman in labor no matter how much she hurt me and mine. So here I am."

Lillie hugged her. "You're a good Christian woman," she said. "It takes a big heart to overlook the kind of hurt you've had."

She saw Vinnie arch her back on the bed. "We'd better get back in there," she said to Judith.

When the pain subsided, Judith said, "It's getting good daylight. I know you need to see about the needs of the rest of your family. I'll be fine by myself with her. I'll call you when we need you again."

"Well, I hate to leave you alone but I'll just go get my household situated for the day and come back. Ida can cook breakfast. Vinnie has been so good for a first baby." She patted Vinnie's shoulder as she talked and the girl relaxed a little. "I'll be right out here in the other room if you need me."

Still struggling for breath, Vinnie said, "Where's Jed?"

"He's sitting at the kitchen table drinking coffee with his Pa." Laughing a little, she continued, "I don't know how strong the coffee is. Matt made it."

Vinnie smiled weakly just as another contraction grabbed her.

Lillie said softly to Judith, "Maybe I'd better not leave. They're coming closer together now."

"No," Judith said, "you go on. We'll be all right."

Lillie eased the door closed behind her just as Ben and Holt burst in from the dugout.

Looking around, Ben said, "What's going on?"

Jed answered before their mother had a chance. "The baby. It started about one o'clock."

Holt's excited voice cut in, "And you didn't call us?"

Grinning, Lillie looked from one to the other. It's a thrilling time for all of us, she thought. But these boys don't need to be here, especially Holt.

She breathed a sigh of relief when she heard Matt say, "Ben, you and Holt go get the outside chores done so we can be in the field right after breakfast. We'll be late as it is but this is a special day."

"Yes," Lillie agreed. "I'll get Ida up and she can have breakfast ready when you get back. Jed, you carry Betsy and lay her on our bed. Maybe she'll sleep a while longer."

Matt said, "I'll just walk out with you boys and check on things."

Ida jumped up and grabbed her clothes and disappeared behind the quilt screen as soon as she saw that the men had all left the room. Coming out dressed, she said, "I thought they'd never leave so I could get up."

Lillie smiled. Seems like everything makes me happy this morning, she thought. My first grandchild is about to make an appearance. To Ida, she said, "I knew your Pa would take care of that. Now, I don't know how soon I'll have to go back to Vinnie so we'll work together on breakfast as long as we can."

The household had assembled with the exception of Betsy by the time they had cooked breakfast. "I'll go send Judith out to eat with you," Lillie said.

But Judith insisted that Lillie eat with her family. "I'll wait until everything is over in here," she said. "I can relax better then."

They had just finished the meal when they heard Vinnie scream. Lillie jumped up from the table. "Ida," she said, "you go to Betsy. If she wakes up, take her outside."

A silent communication with Matt prompted him to scrape his chair back from the table and say, "Come on, Boys, y'all go to the field. Jed, I'll wait outside with you. The women will call us when you're a father."

Lillie returned to Vinnie's bedroom just in time. One more push and Jed's baby entered this vale of tears with a lusty yell.

"Oh, thank goodness," Judith breathed.

Lillie smiled at her in spite of all the work that remained to be accomplished. I'm wearing a continuous smile on my face this day, she thought. And why not? My first grandchild looks complete and healthy.

Vinnie lay exhausted and unspeaking after the birth. Lillie wanted to let her rest at least until she caught her breath but Judith tried to initiate a conversation with her. Vinnie ignored her until she asked if they had named the baby.

"What is it?" Vinnie asked.

"Oh, my goodness, I haven't even told her that it's a boy."

Lillie's smile extended to her voice. "Yes, you have a fine, healthy baby boy," she said.

"Junior," Vinnie managed to say between gasps.

"But I've never heard of anyone not naming the first boy after his Pa's father," Judith said.

Vinnie persisted. "Junior," she said.

Judith didn't give up. She leaned over and whispered to Lillie, "We'll ask Jed."

A tone of finality emanated from the bed. "Junior."

Judith said, "Lillie, you cut the cord and take this boy and clean him up so his Pa can see him. I'll finish up in here."

Lillie put her arms around Judith. "You're the most thoughtful person I know," she said. "There's no way we can ever thank you."

"Pshaw, it's no more than any neighbor would have done. I'm just glad she had an easy time."

Vinnie snorted.

CHAPTER 3

Ben

Two hours later, Ben Conover walked through the woods to Flora's house. Plez's uncle, Stump McIntosh, had let them move into his own home when he and his family moved to eastern Oklahoma. Abby, Stump's wife, had testified at the hearing for the Sexton brothers, Al and Camp, after they had been arrested for the murder of Paul Conover. The very act of testifying had so unnerved the woman that she felt a driving need to live near her own kin. Because a finding of insufficient evidence precluded a further trial on the count of murder, the men had been released on bail pending trial for horse stealing and Abby feared for her life.

Ben found Plez and Flora sitting at their kitchen table drinking coffee. Flora turned around in her chair, snagged a cup from the cabinet, and filled it from the pot sitting on a trivet in the middle of the table.

"It's hot," she said. "We just took it off the stove."

Ben glanced around the one-room cabin as he always did when entering this home. And it is a home, he thought. Flora had brightened it with embroidered scarves on dresser and cabinet tops and crocheted antimacassars on chair backs and arms. Her friendship quilt covered the bed that occupied one corner and took up a fourth of the space in the small room. Turning a dining chair from the living area, he dragged it to the table and straddled it.

"How are things at home?" Flora asked.

Ben hadn't seen them since Jed had moved home. They knew, of course, that the couple had come back to live with them. Matt had told them the first day. It seems like he can't get enough of visiting Flora and Plez since they made up, Ben mused. It's like he's trying to make up for lost time. I think he makes excuses so he can come over here every day. He had expected Flora to wander over but so far she hadn't made it.

He decided to tease them a little and not tell about the baby right away. In fact, he still couldn't believe that Jed had let him be the bearer of the good news and hadn't worked out a good story yet. He let his coffee cool while he thought about it and replied to Flora's question instead.

"Not good," he said. "This thing with Jed and Vinnie living there is just not working out. We tried to figure out the best place for them to sleep, but nothing suits her. First we said they could have the dugout, but she's afraid to be underground. So we set up a bed in the front room for Ida and Betsy and let them have your old room. You can imagine how that sat with Ida."

Pouring cream into his coffee, he stirred it and took a sip. "If there's any more coffee in the pot, you'd better put it back on the stove," he said. "This is getting cool."

Plez lifted the coffeepot, set it on the stove, and poked up the fire before he sat back down.

When did he start doing woman's work? Ben thought, and immediately chastised himself. I sound just like Vinnie, he thought. "Flossie, I didn't mean to be critical. This cup of coffee is just right to drink. But Vinnie has got all of us on edge all the time. Nothing ever pleases her. And she speaks her mind without hesitation. I feel so sorry for Jed."

"Maybe it's her condition, Ben. When the baby comes, she'll probably get over it," Flora said.

"I hope so but I don't bank on it. I remember how much work a new baby can be. And everybody in the house will lose sleep, too. Holt and I will be better off sleeping in the dugout; at least we'll get our rest."

"But little babies are so sweet," Flora said. "They more than make up for all the work. Just think, this will be Ma and Pa's first grandchild. I'm so anxious for it to get here. I'm making a little dress. I wish I knew whether it will be a boy or a girl. But it won't matter; it'll wear dresses for a long time."

Plez laid his arm across the back of Flora's chair and squeezed her shoulder. She favored him with a dazzling smile.

"Am I missing something here?" Ben asked. "I feel like I just left the room."

Flora blushed as Plez chuckled. "We want you to be the first to know, Brother Ben," he said. "You're going to an uncle twice over."

Ben stood and reached across the table to shake his brother-in-law's hand. Then he walked around and kissed Flora giving her a swift hug. "That's great news," he said as he returned to his chair. "Plez, let me tell you about the first time I ever saw your wife. She had entered this world during the night. She had this fuzz of fine, silky hair and the softest skin I ever felt before or since. I stroked her cheek and, when I laid my finger in her hand, her fingers curled right around it. Right around my heart, too. Is it any wonder we have always been so close?"

How different their news is from Jed's shameful hurry-up wedding, he thought. I felt so sorry for him and so helpless at the same time. He made his bed and it's full of briars. But I still feel sorry for him and wish I could help him.

He voiced the thought.

Flora said, "It's Ma I pity. Having a rank stranger suddenly thrust into your household would be bad enough. But knowing that she needs to treat her like a daughter is enough to throw her back into her spells. I think we need to figure out some way to get them out of there. I'd take them myself, but you can see we hardly have room for the two of us. And with a baby coming on…" Her voice trailed off.

The three of them sat lost in thought.

Plez broke the silence. "We can build them a house."

Flora said, "Where?"

Ben hesitated a few minutes before he said, "I have eighty acres. Surely we can find a spot somewhere on it." He felt excitement bubble up in him. "We could put it somewhere far enough away that we wouldn't have to see her."

Flora giggled then sobered. "Ben," she said, "you'll want a house of your own some of these days."

"Flossie." Plez's voice held a warning. "I thought we agreed not to push it."

"I know, but I can't stand to see two people I love so much so unhappy. I have a feeling Ben and Esther will wind up together, so what are we waiting for?"

"Sis, Plez is right. I'm not that unhappy myself because I determined to give Esther a year to get over Jed before I said anything to her. She's getting better all the time, isn't she?"

Flora pursed her lips. "I don't know. Sometimes she seems like her old self and other times she mopes around."

Plez's eyes passed a silent signal to his wife as he said, "Okay, Flora. It's Ben's call anyway. We'll all wait until he gives us the nod. Let's get on with plans to build a house for Jed."

Ben nodded and said, "I think they'll go for it but we need to make sure. We'll put it to them like this; 'We want to be able to see each other's smoke of a morning but not be within hollering range.' And she certainly knows how to holler."

He sobered. "It would be a big job, but now's the time to do it before the crops come up. Pa and Jed and Holt can pitch in. Plez, have you given up on building your own house?"

"We have for right now. With the baby coming and all, we've decided to stay here for the time being. Besides, I still have a lot of work to do clearing the site. In fact, I'm willing to donate the logs I've already cut if we need them for a quick job."

Ben finished his cup of coffee, rose, and reached for his hat. "Oh, I almost forgot to tell you," he said with a sheepish grin. "Vinnie had the baby this morning."

Flora's reaction exceeded Ben's hopes. She sat perfectly still for a moment with a stunned expression on her face. Then she jumped up and reached across the table with fingers curled as if she would choke Ben. "You Imp," she said. "You waited all this time to tell me. I could choke you. What is it? What did they name it? How much did it weigh?"

"Whoa, slow down," Ben said. "One question at a time. They named him Jedidiah Christian Conover, Junior. And I don't know how much he weighed."

Flora glowed. "A little *boy*. I can't wait to see him. Do you suppose it will be all right if we go home with you now?"

"Sure," Ben said. "Jed's the proudest Papa you ever saw. He's just waiting to show him off."

"I wish I had the little dress finished to give them right now," Flora said. "At least I know which way to lap it in the back for a boy. I'm glad I haven't made the buttonholes yet."

❧   ❧   ❧

Jed's enthusiasm for the house project revived the spirits of everyone at home. Ida remarked to Ben that Vinnie even smiled once. Lillie's face bore a happy look and Betsy skipped around the room with such abandon that her mother sent her outside.

Ben and Jed went that very day to walk over Ben's acreage seeking a location for the house. The land rose and then flattened a little north of the pecan grove. Ben had thought of building his own house on the site but quickly decided that Jed's immediate need outweighed any nebulous future plans of his own. After all, he thought, I don't even have a wife or a hope of one. My dreams might not pan out no matter how important they are to me.

While Jed and Plez worked cutting trees and Holt trimmed off the small limbs with a hatchet and piled them to be burned later, Ben and Matt went to the lumberyard to make arrangements for credit. Ben wanted to use native stone for the fireplace and logs for the walls but would need materials for floor, windows and roof. After seeing the estimate for shingles and nails, for tongue-and-groove flooring, 2x4s for rafters, 1x4s for lath and window frames, Ben decided to make his own doors.

Matt said, "Son, you'll need to pay for lumber to make doors and jambs and they won't be as weather-tight. I suggest you go ahead and get millwork doors. I think you'll regret it if you don't."

Embarrassed, Ben pulled his father aside. "But, Pa, it's running a lot more than I thought it would. I don't see how I can pay for it."

"Have you thought about cutting down some place else, say, leave off the flooring? Lots of people live on dirt floors."

"I sure hate to do that, especially with a baby. We'll have to think about it."

"Thank you for the estimate," he told the lumberman. "We're just getting started on the house and don't need supplies right now. If we need more credit than this estimate, do you think you might help us out?" Ben's stomach knotted at having to ask. It had been such a short time since he had borrowed money to buy his land. Now he bargained to incur debt in order to build a house on the land. I won't even be living in the house, he thought. Will I have the money for a home of my own some day?

"I'm willing to run you a bill for this amount with your Pa standing good for it. As far as I can see, you are good, honest people and I believe you'll pay your bills. But if it takes any more than this, I'll have to put a lien on the house. I hate to cloud the title but I need to protect myself. I'll release it when you pay it off."

Ben breathed a sigh of relief but determined to save every penny he could in building costs.

CHAPTER 4

Jed

Jed worked from daylight till dark on his house. As the days lengthened into early summer and the work in the fields filled his days, he carried a lantern to his house after dark trying to finish the inside enough that he could move in with Vinnie and the baby. Vinnie always wanted to go with him but he didn't think it a good idea. As long as the baby stayed where they laid him, he didn't worry. But when the baby began to roll over, they had no clean place to put him. And Jed didn't know what age that might be. He knew his boy outshone other babies of the same age. Ben had decided that he couldn't afford a wood floor and Jed saw no other spot than the dirt floor available to put the infant.

He felt two ways about it, though. It seemed that he had no time to spend with the little fellow. Vinnie chopped cotton alongside him during the day leaving J. C. with his grandmother. They had started out calling him Junior but one day while Ida played with him she called him by his initials and swore he smiled at her. From then on they all adopted the new name.

Vinnie went to the house to feed him during the time that Lillie cooked the meals. Lillie had suggested it so that she might teach Vinnie something about cooking. Hiram Wade had exacted so much farm labor from his daughters that they had little time to learn domestic duties. Mrs. Wade had feared her husband, too, and did not insist on teaching the girls.

Vinnie was not a quick study. Lillie told Jed one day in exasperation, "Son, I shouldn't say it, but after you move out to yourself, you come by and eat with us when you get hungry."

Jed felt uncomfortable. "Ma, we'll do all right. I know Vinnie is a little backward but she's a hard worker and she loves little J. C. and me. If you can just show her how to make bread, I can fill up on that and milk." He hugged her and wished he could make her smile. "Pa promised to loan old Bossy to us but you know how she hates for me to milk her. If I can just get her to give down her milk I won't starve."

It didn't get a rise out of her. "Son, you have always had the biggest appetite of any of my children," she said. "I won't stop worrying about you until you promise me you'll let me feed you sometimes."

"Okay, Ma. I think I can get by with it if it's something Vinnie hasn't learned to cook yet. You make some of the best things, like light bread and jelly. I don't think Vinnie would mind getting to eat some of that good hot bread and butter and your plum jelly herself."

Each night after supper, Ida and Ben insisted that he go to work on his house while they did the evening chores. He and Vinnie took J. C. with them and laid him on a quilt near the small garden that Vinnie had spaded up. She planted beans, cucumbers, okra, black-eyed peas, tomatoes, and cantaloupe and talked of big plans to enlarge the area and make a fall garden. She said that she wished she could have started early enough to have spring vegetables but her confinement prevented that. She alternately frowned and smiled when she said it because she thought J. C. surely made up for it.

They got into an argument about putting J. C. on the dirt floor. Jed agreed to put the baby outside on the grass but decided that the bare earth in the house got the quilt too dirty. He determined to send Vinnie and the baby home.

She balked. "You don't know what it's like for me up there with your folks when you're not there," she said. Her voice rose a notch. "I can tell they don't like me. Oh, they try to be nice, everyone but Ida. She says everything that comes to her mind. I know I'm not welcome so I don't say anything back no matter what she says. I had enough practice at that living with Pa. If it wasn't for J. C. they wouldn't tolerate me."

Jed knew it to be true but he felt like arguing. "That ain't so. Vinnie, I think you're making a mountain out of a molehill. Ma is doing her best to help you learn the things you didn't learn at home." He saw her face flush and shuddered at the thought of getting into a big argument. Changing the subject, he said, "But that's not the problem right now. I just don't want you to get that quilt dirty. Ma loaned it to us and you know washing it all the time will wear it out. Now, go on and let me get back to work."

"If I just had a cradle or a bed to lay J. C. down on, I could help you. When are you going to build him one?"

I started something, Jed thought. I'll never get any work done if we get to fussing again. But he couldn't help himself. "Look, Vinnie," he said. "I work in the fields all day and at night I break my back trying to finish this house. When do you think I have time to make a bed?" I'd better make up with her before we go at it tooth and nail, though, he thought. He went to her and put his arms around her. "I want our own home as much as you do. I just think it best for J. C. if you take him up to the folks so you can put him to bed and get some sleep yourself. I never know how late I'll work. If I get a job started sometimes I work until I can see a good stopping spot."

"I never get to see you any more." She began to sniffle.

She's trying to pick a fight, he thought. He snapped back. "Don't *see* me? We both work in the fields all day long and you never get to see me?"

"You know what I mean. Somebody else is always there except when you come in at night and you're asleep as soon as your head hits the pillow."

This will never get us anywhere, he thought, I'll see if I can mollify her. "I've been thinking about building a bed for J. C.," he said. "I've about got to where I can see it in my mind but I don't see how I can get hold of the right material since we don't have any ready cash. We've been sponging off the folks long enough but I don't see what else we can do."

Vinnie interrupted him. "It's not like we lay around like my sisters' husbands. We help out as much as we can."

"Yeah, but we need to be out on our own. I think I'll talk to Pa and see what he thinks about me trying to hire out to some other farmer. It's not long till school is out and Holt will make another hand."

Vinnie shifted the sleeping baby to one arm and gathered up the quilt. "I can't wait until the day comes when we can move in here," she said.

"We'll just have to try to be content until we can make that happen."

When Jed got home around midnight, Vinnie had waited up for him. She ran to him and hugged him as she bubbled over. "Look what I'm doing," she said. "I told your Ma that we didn't have anywhere to lay J. C. in the house and she suggested that we make a rug for the floor. She got up right that minute and started digging out old worn-out clothes she had been saving. She said, 'If you keep anything for seven years you'll find a use for it.' And she gave me this tubfull to tear up to make a rag rug. She's going to show me how and help me finish it fast."

She had talked so fast that she had to stop for breath.

Jed breathed a sigh of relief. He walked around the table to the stove and checked the warming oven. Finding a plate of cornbread, he set it on the table.

"Do you want me to make a pot of coffee?" Vinnie asked.

Jed sat down. "No, get me some sweet milk in a goblet. I'll just eat milk and bread." It's nice, he thought, to have a chance to eat a bite before bed. Most nights I just crawl into bed when I get home.

Vinnie set the glass of milk in front of him and sat opposite. He fished a spoon from the holder in the middle of the table and crumbled cornbread into the milk. After he devoured several bites he slowed down enough to talk.

"I got to thinking about that floor after you left. I think I'll start on it next. We've got a pretty good pile of rocks that we dug up to prepare the fields. I think Pa will be glad to get rid of them. I'd been figuring on using them to build the fireplace, though. I don't think there's enough for both. I almost had my mind set to build the fireplace clear across the north end of the house. I may have to make it smaller or quarry more rock. That's such a back-breaking job that I hate to think about it."

Vinnie said, "I could help you."

"No, that's a man's job. You'd hurt yourself."

"I've done a man's work since I was knee high to a jack rabbit."

Jed reached across the table and took her hand. She had piled part of the old clothes on the table and torn them into strips as they talked. The sound had grated on Jed's ears until he thought he would scream. "Clean up your work and let's go to bed," he said.

During the night the rain set in. When they checked the sky the next morning, Matt told them, "It looks like it will rain all day; we won't work in the field today."

Jed said, "Pa, I'd like to talk to you about the rock we piled up when we cleared the land. I'd like to use it in my house if you don't have a use for it."

Matt said, "Truth to tell, I'll be glad to get rid of it. It attracts mice and rats and other little varmints. Looks like today will be a good day to load it and haul it to your place. I didn't think you'd be ready to start your fireplace, though."

"I'm thinking about laying a stone floor. We hate to put J. C. down on dirt."

Matt and Ben exchanged a look. Matt said, "There's not near enough rock for both. We don't have a fireplace here. What you need to do is find you a stove. You'll need a cook stove, anyway."

"I don't have the money to buy a stove right now. I can fix it so Vinnie can cook in the fireplace. What I thought I'd do is separate out the stones according to their best use. If Ben will let me, I'll quarry stone on that rocky hill in the northeast corner of his place."

"Sure," Ben said, "but that's going to take a lot of time. Will you have enough time to get the stone ready, lay a floor, and build a fireplace before winter comes? I can help when it's raining like it is today but we need to make a crop of cotton and enough corn and hay to get the animals through the winter."

Jed turned to Matt. "Pa, I need to make some money. What do you think of me trying to hire out to some farmer?"

"You do what you need to do," Matt said. "We'll get along. Holt will be out of school tomorrow. He's making quite a man; he can take your place. If you want to go today, I'll loan you my slicker."

Jed didn't know how to go about looking for a job but he thought he knew just the person to ask. He hurried to saddle Blaze and rode over to the Wilson place. Polly came to the door to tell him that her father had left a little early that morning. "You'll find him at the store, I'm sure," she said.

In Chagris, Baxter Wilson scratched his chin as he told Jed, "I haven't had anybody tell me that they need hands so far this year. The county has about finished the roads in this section so they're not hiring as far as I know. I wish I had better news; I'll keep you in mind and recommend you. I know you'll make a good hand for somebody."

Disappointed, Jed thought about riding to some of the other towns but rejected the idea. I wouldn't know how to go about working in a store, he thought, and anybody that needs a farm hand will want to hire someone they know. He let Blaze walk back to his Pa's place.

Ben came out of the barn to meet him. Rain soaked his clothing and dripped from his hair. "Any luck?" he asked.

"No. I talked to Mr. Wilson and he didn't give me any hope. You're a sight, you know that? I'll go pull off this slicker so you can use it."

"No, once you get soaking wet it doesn't bother you so much." Ben's face softened but his tone of voice teased. "Looks like you didn't get out of the hard work of moving rock, after all," he said. "I'm about finished with the chores; I can help you."

❦   ❦   ❦

The rain didn't let up. Matt told Jed, "You might as well work on your house; we'll take care of the chores. If this rain keeps on, we'll lose the crops, anyway."

Jed trudged doggedly to his house each morning. Mud gummed the soles of his high-top shoes threatening to pull them off even though he had tied them as tightly as he could. Topsoil had washed away in many places exposing the red clay underneath. Slipping and sliding on those places almost caused him to fall. He cut a sturdy branch to make a walking stick for assistance.

Ben slogged over every day after finishing the chores. Together they lifted heavy rocks and laid them on the makeshift worktable Jed had fashioned. While Jed chiseled and chipped the limestone to make the size and shape stone that he wanted, Ben chinked the inside walls of the log house.

Red clay for chinking material abounded; making it thick enough proved to be a problem. Jed told Ben, "Just work inside the house and drain the water from mixing the clay onto the floor. I'm going to cover it up, anyhow."

After a few days of continuing steady rain, Jed checked the rocky hill in the northeast corner of Ben's land. Rivulets had turned into streams washing some of the clay down into the creek that ran down the edge of Ben's land and through Matt's acreage. With more rock exposed, Jed could see the thickness of the strata. I don't know how to separate it out, he thought. If I have to use this rock, I'll have to learn more than I know now. Despite a keen desire to finish the dwelling, he dreaded even the thought of all the hard work of quarrying rock. I wish I could find some other way, he thought. I wish I had some money.

He stood a while looking at the rock picturing his fireplace plan in his mind. This stone here is the perfect thickness for the mantle, he thought. If I could just get it out in one piece…. Taking a chisel from his back pocket, he began cleaning the remaining dirt at the end of the exposed limestone. As he uncovered more stone and found that one layer extended for several feet, he became more excited. When he came to the fissure marking the end, he stepped down onto the next level of the hill and surveyed the stone, calculating its length. It must be eight feet long, he exulted. I wonder who I can find to teach me how to quarry it.

CHAPTER 5

Ben

Ben went home early each day to start the chores. Holt and his sisters liked to go to the barn with him. It got them away from the worsening tension of being cooped up in the house and coping with Jed's family. A placid baby, as a general rule J. C. gurgled and cooed. But when he took a spell of bawling it lasted a while. They tried passing him from one to the other to see if anyone could pacify him. Ordinarily Vinnie took him to their bedroom to try to feed him and get him to sleep. Sometimes it worked but when it didn't they could still hear him.

Constant rain and unusually cool weather for May had precipitated such an attack of Matt's rheumatism that every movement caused pain. He tried to stay in bed but that seemed to make it worse. The boys convinced him that they could handle the reduced work without him and, although he grumbled, he remained indoors.

Lillie managed to hold her tongue when Ida nipped at Vinnie but increasingly often she stepped out onto the front porch and closed the door after her. Ben thought, Vinnie told Jed she doesn't answer back but that's not true. I feel sorry for her but she could be a little more co-operative. I'm just glad I can go to the dugout every night to sleep.

On the day that Jed checked the rocky hill, Ben sloshed his way home, shoes squeaking with every step. The creek that ran east of his acreage curved onto his Pa's place. Banks filled to the brim with rainfall and runoff made it necessary to use the old footbridge near his father's homestead. That required nearly three-quarters of a mile walk between the two houses. When Ben reached the

footbridge that afternoon he couldn't see it and only found it by the path leading to it on each side indicating its location. Murky red water spread out onto
the surrounding area having risen a few inches during the day.

To the north of their cotton field on the west side of the creek, a stand of
blackjack timber screened Jed's location from view. The two men had chosen a
flat space away from the creek for the dwelling. Although the incessant rain
had carved new washes in the land, it flowed downward to the creek from the
house place. At the present time crossing the creek presented no danger but
Ben feared that if Jed worked until near dark his trip home would be risky. He
saw no way to warn Jed other than to trudge back to hollering distance.

He wished he had time to cut a pole to stake out the location of the bridge
but that would require a walk to the woods and back. Instead he turned and
retraced his steps. As soon as he thought Jed could hear him, he cupped his
hands into a makeshift megaphone and yelled as loudly as he could. Jed had his
back turned toward the sound and gave no indication that he heard it. Ben put
two fingers in his mouth and whistled. After several times of moving forward a
few steps and stopping to whistle, he made enough noise that Jed heard him
and looked over his shoulder.

Ben's frantic gesturing brought Jed to his feet. He dropped his tools on the
table and started trying to run toward Ben. Oh, no, Ben thought, his tools
could rust or wash away before we can come back over here. He raised his arms
and waved them in a cross above his head until Jed stopped. Ben plodded
closer until Jed could hear him.

"Bring your tools," he yelled. "We have to get back before the bridge washes
out."

Cloudy skies and rain that came down in sheets hastened nightfall. Daylight
faded until they had a hard time seeing by the time they reached the footbridge, a rickety affair of three 2x12s cleated on each end and in the middle. It
had been laid across the deepest part of the creek where the banks were per-
pendicular on each side. During dry weather with low water in the creek, children liked to bounce on the bridge and, if they fell in, no real harm befell them.
After several days of rain, however, the banks had softened and offered less
support.

Ben and Jed decided to take off their shoes so they could feel for the unseen
bridge with their feet. As he tied the strings together and slung the muddy
shoes around his neck, Jed said, "I've been wet and dirty so long a little more
mud won't hurt me."

Ben stepped gingerly into the water, feeling for the bridge. Jed, impatient as usual, said, "You'll never get across at this rate. Here, let me go first." He waded quickly into the water at the end of the visible path. After a few steps, he said, "I can feel the bridge. Come on."

When Ben touched the bridge, he steadied himself on one foot and probed with the other until he found both edges. Making sure that he walked on the center board, he started across. Jed had reached the middle of the bridge by that time. He turned to check on Ben and lost his footing. Throwing his arms out for balance too late, he tried in vain to right himself. He went completely under the water and came up sputtering.

Ben burst out laughing. "You need any help?"

"These brogans are pulling me back under," Jed said. "If you can reach me and take them, I can swim out."

By the time they reached home, Jed began to see the comical side of the situation. "Boy, can't we get into some messes," he said.

"Well, at least you can,"Ben said, joining in Jed's laughter. "We'd better straighten up and go to the dugout to see if we can find some dry clothes before we go in the house. Let's wash up as best we can at the horse trough first."

Still barefoot, Ben led the way down the dugout steps. When he stepped off the last one, water covered his foot. "Uh-oh," he said, "the water's coming up in here. We're going to have to carry everything out to save it. I don't know where we'll put it; we'd better go tell Pa."

Lillie took over to direct the move. "Take all the canned goods to the house and set them behind the stove," she told them. "Move the empty jars on the top shelves after you remove all the full ones." They formed a line and began passing the food up the dugout stairs as if they were a bucket brigade. "We don't have much canned goods left over," Lillie said. "We'll need every bit of it if the gardens wash out."

Vinnie wailed from the top step where she had been handing jars to Ida, "Will my garden be gone?" She tramped down the stairs until she could duck her head inside and see Jed. "What's happening to my garden?"

"It hasn't washed away yet but the way this rain is keeping up with the ground so soaked, we may not save it."

"Can't you go back over there and build a dam around it?"

"No, I can't," Jed said. "I already fell in the creek once. Now go get back in line and let's get back to work." He handed another jar to Holt as Vinnie pushed her way past Ben on the middle step.

"I guess we'll have to put up a bed for the girls in our bedroom," Lillie said when she saw that they had the food transfer well under way. "Let me talk to Matt and see what he says."

The next morning their cotton fields nearest the creek lay under water. However, they had built the house on higher land. Matt said he thought it would remain dry unless they had the flood of the century. Sheds and barn north of the residence were on a level with it. However, water overflowed the access lane between the dwelling and the fields.

"We can get out if we just have to," Matt said. "But I see no reason to panic."

"I wonder if Flora is all right," Lillie worried. "I wish I could see her place but those trees hide it."

"Now, Lillie," Matt said, "don't borrow trouble. If they need us, they'll get word to us somehow. Besides, the Wilson place is up the hill from them; they can go over there if they need to."

"I guess we have enough to worry about keeping body and soul together here," Lillie said. "I just hope we have enough food to last. Maybe my garden won't wash away."

Even when all the children had been home the house seemed more than adequate. Ben considered it a mansion when he compared it to the dwellings that housed their neighbors. Most parents of his acquaintance had raised their children in two rooms, many of them much smaller than their own three-room log house. But, he thought, we had the dugout for overflow. And we didn't have Vinnie.

He tried to cheer everyone up by making humorous remarks but Vinnie looked on the dark side of every situation. Ben thought the rain would never stop but he kept his opinion to himself. Vinnie looked out a window a dozen times a day and said, "This rain will never stop."

Ben got so tired of hearing her say the same thing over and over that he moved one of the dining chairs to the front porch and sat there after he had finished all his chores at the barn. Sometimes his father joined him, but most times Matt just sat in his big chair and turned a deaf ear to the activities of the womenfolk.

Jed and Holt seemed to fare better than anyone else did because they busied themselves making a workbench in the barn. They shared woodworking ability and planned to build furniture for Jed's new house as soon as Jed could afford the material. Ben had tried to help them but decided he got in their way. They didn't say anything to make him feel unwanted but, as he watched them working together as one efficient unit, he felt like he was all thumbs.

Drying clothes proved to be their biggest problem. Ben strung wires in the barn but without heat to hasten the drying time, the heavy cotton garments took more than a day to lose enough moisture that they could be ironed. They didn't have that much time when it came to J. C.'s diapers and resorted to stringing a line behind the range. The inside air smelled of wet diaper all the time even though they raised the windows on the porch side of the main room.

Lillie had him move the wash bench onto the front porch after a couple of days. "I'm glad it's the end of May," she said. "At least, the weather is warmer even though the rain cools if off somewhat."

They set the tubs under the dripline of the porch to fill them with clean water. Lillie told the men to pour out the dirty water off the edge of the porch. "No use getting any wetter than we have to," she said. "My flowers I planted earlier are gone, anyway. We'll be lucky if we save any of the cash crop; I can't worry about flowers."

Ben watched the level of the flood water creep up every day. They couldn't take the cattle and horses to the pasture because it lay in a low place near the creek. In normal times the proximity of the creek enhanced the growth of grass as well as providing a convenient place for the animals to drink. Although Ben could not see the area for the trees that lay between it and the home place, he reckoned the creek level covered all the pasture.

He worried that the hay wouldn't last. The beasts needed more than hay to keep up their strength; they needed grass this time of year. He hoarded the small store of corn for the milk cows, grinding the amount he considered the minimum portion each day. They gave less milk on the decreased rations so he decided to wean their calves. I wouldn't do it, he thought, but the family needs the milk worse.

That arrangement didn't work. Even though Jed reinforced the stalls, the cows kicked at them trying to get to their bawling calves. Agitation decreased their milk supply further. Disappointed, Ben turned them back together and skipped that evening's milking. By the next morning, however, things had returned to normal for the dams and after the morning's milking, he let the calves strip their mothers.

Lillie tried to keep teaching Vinnie to cook. Ben could see his mother's exasperation when Vinnie cooked a meal by herself. Lillie prepared a meal in an organized manner making every move count and cleaning up as she went. Vinnie moved in a slap-dash fashion, slinging things together and leaving the cabinet and stove in a mess. Ida couldn't stand it; she added her suggestions making Vinnie more nervous and testy.

Ben headed for the barn when the women got on his nerves too much. He sat and talked to Jed and Holt, handing them things or straightening nails. He got quite good at holding the point of a used nail and keeping the bend up without letting the nail roll until the crook lay on the surface. Hitting the nail dead center with a hammer flattened it enough that a few small strokes made the nail straight enough to use again. They worked until the ringing dinner bell called them in time for the meal.

Late one afternoon the sun came out lighting the clouds with pink and gold. It sank in a glowing red sky. Matt walked around the corner from the kitchen door smiling. "Red sky at morning, sailors take warning; red sky at night, sailor's delight," he said.

Next day Plez appeared over the crest of the rise south of the house, a fifty-pound sack of flour over his left shoulder and a syrup bucket in his right hand. He had used the old wagon track because the new lane still lay under water.

Ben had been sitting on the porch and ran to meet him relieving him of the flour. "I could hug you," he said as Plez shifted the bucket from his right hand and extended the hand toward Ben. "What's going on? We haven't seen a soul besides just us in over a week."

"Let me get my breath and I'll tell you what I know. Maybe it would be better to get everybody together so I won't have to tell it but once."

Lillie met them at the edge of the porch. "Is Flora all right?"

Plez laughed, a pleasant sound. "Except for mornings, she does fine. I tried to cook breakfast for her, but you know Flora. She'd cook if her head were falling off. And she's been worrying about y'all. Come on in the house and I'll tell you all about it."

Lillie rang the dinner bell long and hard until Jed and Holt appeared in the barn door. They started to the house on a run but when Ben yelled, "Plez is here," they slowed to a fast walk.

Plez went to meet them throwing an arm around each of them. Ben thought, Plez is as much a part of this family as if he had been born into it. I'm so glad Pa went over there and got things straightened out with them. I think Pa is glad, too.

When their household gathered around, everyone started asking questions at the same time. Plez laughed again and held up a hand, palm outward. "Hold on," he said. "Let me tell things in my own way first, then I'll answer questions. All right? I brought copies of *The Ardmoreite* so you can read about some of the bad flooding on the Washita and the Red River. Fourteen people drowned when they took refuge on an island that had formed between the old and new channels of Red River. The water rose so fast that they couldn't get away."

He pulled out several newspapers from under the bib of his overalls and handed them to Matt. "You can read about it for yourself," he said. "North Texas has been hit bad. There's a report in the papers that 50 lives have been lost there, 10 million dollar property loss, 2 million crop loss and 3 million dollar loss to the railroads."

Lillie gasped. "I wonder if all my folks in Texas are all right," she said. "I haven't heard a word from any of them."

Plez sighed. "I'm afraid you won't hear from them for a while. So many bridges have been washed out that the trains can't get through. When Flora and I went on our wedding trip, we passed through a place called the Rock Cut on the Washita north of Ardmore. The railroad tracks through there have been washed away for more than a mile. Now that the rain has stopped, they're hoping to do some repairs and resume train service."

Ben had been listening as Plez told the harrowing stories. His mind had been on Esther ever since the flood began. The McMasters farm lay on higher ground but a creek ran across it and emptied into the creek that extended from his father's acreage across the road and onto Sid Drumm's place. He could stand it no longer.

"Tell us what's happening around here," he said, "and how you managed to get across the creek today."

Plez said, "I used a boat to row across the creek; the bridge is still under water on the main road. A wagon delivered some freight to Pa's store yesterday and he brought some provisions to our neighbors along the section line from Chagris to his place. The bridge over Red Branch is holding and so far the bridge south of this place is, too, but Pa borrowed a boat from one of his customers in town and I used it to bring y'all a few provisions and to see how you're doing. It looks like the water is going down so we may be able to save this bridge but I don't think most of the crops will survive."

"What about the rest of the neighbors?" Ben asked.

Plez shot him a devilish grin. "Well, Sid Drumm's place looks pretty well flooded. Flora and I are doing okay under the circumstances. Pa and Polly are managing. I haven't heard anything about the Pendletons. I aim to go by there on my way back home. And Brother Goodgion is down in bed, I heard. Leon is staying with them. Let's see, is that everybody?"

Ben could have choked him. He didn't mind being teased by Flora and Plez but, if Ida got started, he'd never hear the last of it. But he managed to look Plez in the eye and say in a mild tone, "Almost."

Plez said, "Oh, yeah. I went by the McMasters' on my way here and took them some provisions. Their farmstead is surrounded by high water. The creek on their place that drains into the one that runs through this land is backed up. They're taking it in stride, though. The boys are wading to the barn to take care of the stock and Esther is making summer dresses for her and Mrs. McMasters and Beulah. I guess everybody will be all right unless it's Sid Drumm. His barn and outbuildings have water up on them several feet and his house isn't much better. It's built too close to the creek, I think. I'm afraid his horses will be ruined; I know he has no way of keeping their hooves dry."

Matt said, "He hasn't had anything to do with us since Buford and the Sexton boys stole his horses. I'll try to go over there after the water goes down and see if I can help him. When a man is on the bottom, sometimes he will let even an enemy lift him up."

"I'd go on down there myself but I need to get home before dark," Plez said. "You boys come back to the boat with me. I brought more stuff that I couldn't carry the first trip. Let me hold J. C. once more before I go."

CHAPTER 6

Lillie

Lillie stretched in the sunshine bathing her back yard with its glorious light. She turned in a slow circle inspecting every area of the yard and buildings after their recent drowning from all the rain. She couldn't see the front porch but knew that Vinnie bent over a wash tub there scrubbing clothes. That's one good thing about her, Lillie thought. She's clean and neat as a pin. I'll relieve her in a minute and let her rest a while.

That morning the men had gone to the barn as soon as they ate breakfast. Lillie could see Holt in the distance sitting on a fallen log whittling as he watched the cattle graze. That boy has a knife in his hand every time he sits down, his mother thought.

Matt stood on the edge of the water near the lane that led to the main road. About half the muddy lane lay exposed to the drying sunshine.

Lillie picked her way within hearing distance. "It's going down pretty fast," she said. "How long do you think it will be before we can get out?"

Matt turned and walked back to her side. "A few more days of this sun and wind and I think we can cross over the creek," he said. "The road's going to be muddy for a while longer, though; it will be rough going. It's a good thing Plez brought provisions when he did."

"Yes. I'm anxious to see Flora and find out for myself how she's doing." She patted his back. "How's the lumbago this morning?"

He smiled down at her. "Better, since I got out in the sunshine and moved around a bit," he said. "Well, I'd better go back and help the boys. I left them cleaning out the barn. It's quite a job after the animals have been shut up in there all this time."

Lillie, Vinnie, and Ida had spent all day the day before washing clothes and bed linens, hanging them on every available bush and fence after they filled the clotheslines. That night Lillie had sprinkled clothes until she filled a wash tub with them. After clearing the breakfast dishes Ida had put the sad irons on the range to heat and laid the ironing board across two ladder-back chairs. I'll check on her before I take my turn at the scrub board, Lillie thought. I wonder what day of the month it is; must be after the first of June by now. It's easier to keep up with the days of the week than the day of the month. I've missed worship two Sundays; this must be Thursday. Maybe it will dry up enough to go this Sunday, if not, at least the Sunday after next.

Her hopes were dashed when she looked out the window the next morning. Instead of receding farther, the creek had risen, and rather than spread out on the surrounding land, the water moved swiftly. As she watched, she saw the footbridge west of their place hurtling down the creek, twisting and bobbing as it passed out of sight.

Matt said, "Something has broken loose up the creek from us. It must be a dam of some sort." Since their arrival over a year before, not one of them had traveled more than a few miles north of their homestead.

"It looks like we're isolated again," Ben said.

The disappointment in his voice brought out Lillie's motherly instincts. "We're no worse off than at the beginning since Plez brought food to us. We'll make out all right."

She didn't believe it, though. Without knowing how long the flood would last, she determined to apportion the remaining provisions carefully for each day. They had an ample supply of eggs, milk, and butter but her bunch devoured bread and meat each meal. Canned vegetables and fruit could be stretched to last another few weeks; they should have been eating food from the garden by now. But if the gardens washed away, they must replant and hope for the best.

Gloom marked the faces of every member of the family when they sat down to the noon meal. Lillie tried to lighten the mood by asking Betsy to tell about her morning, but before the child said a word Vinnie's whiny voice interrupted, "What are we going to do? We'll never see the end of this water, water everywhere."

Lillie hid her smile, certain that Vinnie had never heard of *The Rhyme of the Ancient Mariner*. Comparing their situation with an albatross around the neck, she decided she would choose the cross they had been bearing for more than a week and that threatened to last much longer with more damage.

Lillie made sure she had the attention of each of her children before she said to Vinnie, "We'll bear up under this as well as we can. I expect all of you to do your part and not complain. If we knew how long this would last, we could make better plans. Since we don't know, we will have to ration the food we have left. I'll decide how much to prepare for each meal. If you are still hungry, you can find plenty of milk to drink. We'll have a big breakfast of eggs every day and that should tide us over." There, she thought, that should make everyone sit up and take notice without hurting Vinnie's feelings.

However, she could tell that Vinnie didn't like it. I'm not going to take a word of what I said back, she thought. I may not be able to keep her from complaining but she might as well learn how to fit in with this family. Besides, I don't want J. C. affected by her attitude. If necessary, I'll have a talk with Jed. I think he can handle her.

After dinner the men all disappeared outside. Lillie told Vinnie, "Let's get out your rug you've been working on and see if we can begin to sew it together. Maybe having a project to keep us busy will make the time pass faster."

Vinnie smiled for the first time that day. "I've got a lot of the braiding done but I don't know how to finish it up. I could use some help there." Handing J. C. to Ida she said, "I'll go get it."

Lillie tried not to become exasperated when she saw Vinnie's large stitches. This girl can't even thread a needle, she thought; Betsy could do better. Then she reminded herself of Vinnie's lack of training in even the smallest household skills. I must be more patient with her, she thought. She does try hard.

Lillie had planned to prepare supper early this day, but hearing the mantle clock strike three, she decided to wait a while longer.

Betsy had been walking the floor and stopping to look out different windows, walking around the room and advancing window by window until she finished the circuit of the five windows in the room. Her tramping rhythm as she completed several laps grated on Lillie's frayed nerves and she considered calling her down. Suddenly the child started jumping up and down. "Someone is coming, someone is coming," she said.

Lillie and Vinnie dropped their work and went to the window to see for themselves. A bedraggled man and woman struggled through the driving rain across the muddy approach from the old trail. Each of them staggered crookedly as they shifted back and forth to balance the heavy sacks tied across their shoulders and falling below their outstretched arms. In addition, they each carried sacks in both hands.

Ida, who had been in Jed and Vinnie's room trying to get J. C. to sleep, appeared carrying the baby and joined them. "That's Mr. and Mrs. Drumm," she said. "Man alive, they must be toting everything they've got." Handing the baby to his mother, she said, "I'll go tell Pa."

The three boys beat their father around the house. However, when they recognized the couple, they slid to a fast halt and waited for Matt to catch up. Lillie thought, I hadn't realized how much his rheumatism has slowed him down. She saw him walk toward the couple and knew they had some sort of conversation although she couldn't hear them.

Matt beckoned to his boys who hurried forward and relieved the pair of their burdens. He led them to the front porch.

Lillie could hear him now. "If you'll wait here until I can tell my wife, I'd appreciate it. I won't be long."

Lillie waited with trepidation. Seeing the load they had been carrying, she surmised that they had brought as many of their worldly possessions as they could carry. The couple had neither spoken to them nor had acted in any neighborly way since Buford had been involved in stealing their horses. I don't blame them, Lillie thought. They must be in dire straits to come here now.

Matt closed the door behind him when he entered. "Lillie," he said, "the Drumms have been forced out of their place by the high water. I know we're about as crowded as we can stand, but I can't turn them down."

Lillie tried to put a name to his tone of voice. He knows I'll be the one to bear the brunt of keeping any more people but he's still in charge. He could have brought them in here without consulting me but he's trying his best to make our marriage a partnership again. Dismay filled her mind as she looked around the crowded room and thought of the small store of provisions that she would have to stretch to feed two more. Looking at Matt's face with questions written all over it, she put a smile on her own.

"Of course you can't," she said. "Let's not leave them waiting out on the porch."

Vinnie wailed. "Where are we going to put them? They can't have our room."

Lillie felt like slapping her. "When people have no place else to go, our family will take them in," she said to Vinnie. Her icy voice and choice of words caused the young woman to grab her baby and retreat to her bedroom.

She heard the screen door close and saw Matt leading the couple into the room. Scanning their faces as she stepped forward to meet them, she guessed them to be in their mid-fifties, somewhere between her age and Matt's. Weather-beaten skin on both of them as well as the woman's drawn and wrinkled face may have caused them to look older, but Lillie doubted it.

Afraid to offer her hand for fear of being rebuffed, she smiled and said, "Welcome."

Matt introduced the couple. "Lillie, I don't believe you have met Mr. and Mrs. Drumm. My wife, Lillie."

Lillie nodded to Sid Drumm while she wondered about Mrs. Drumm's given name. Well, plenty of time for that later. We may not ever get past formal names. "Come in, come in," she said. "Have a seat while we get acquainted. Do you drink coffee? I'll put on a fresh pot."

Matt saw the couple seated in ladderback chairs near the dining table. Their clothing dripped from the rain and clung to their skinny bodies. The short, scrawny man might be able to wear some of the boy's clothes stored in a trunk in the loft, Lillie thought. But the woman's height ruled out the possibility that she could wear any of the women's clothes without embarrassment. My skirts wouldn't fall much below her knees, Lillie thought. We'll have to sew a ruffle on one of them.

Aloud, she said, "If we can find anything you can wear, we need to get you into some dry clothes. We can wring yours out and hang them behind the stove and they should be wearable before long."

Neither of the couple had made a sound since they came into the room. At her offer, Sid looked at her directly for the first time. "That's mighty kind of you, Ma'am," he said. "But we've been wet so long it seems sort of normal."

His wife scowled but said nothing. Lillie chose to sympathize with the grimace and ignore the polite refusal. "Mr. Drumm," she said, "you gentlemen are made of sterner stuff than ladies. I'm afraid we women like our creature comforts."

Beckoning to Ida, she said, "I'm going to take Mrs. Drumm to our bedroom and see what we can do about getting her more comfortable. I want you to start supper. I've had red beans soaking on the back of the stove. Build a little fire and simmer them for an hour or two before you make the cornbread." She sighed. "I wish we had better to offer our company than that, but with butter and milk, and canned peaches for dessert, we'll have to make do."

Mrs. Drumm spoke for the first time. "It'll be a feast for us. We ain't eat hot food for days."

Lillie grabbed a folded towel from a bureau in the front room before she led her guest to her bedroom. "We'll get you dried off and find something for you to put on," she said. "I think my clothes will fit you except for the length. You can slip behind that tall dresser across the corner there to change."

Mrs. Drumm remained quiet. She says less than any woman I ever saw, Lillie thought. In response, she found herself chattering to fill the emptiness.

"I have one skirt in mind. It's print and I wear a solid waist with it. I'm sure I have some of the solid material left that I can make a flounce to piece out the skirt so it'll be long enough."

Mrs. Drumm still had not said anything and stood awkwardly in the center of the room. An occasional drop of water dribbled from her skirt onto the rug. She must be miserable, Lillie thought, I'll hurry and get the ruffle sewed on.

"I hate to ask you to stand but, as you can see, we don't have any seats in here but my little sewing rocker. And I'm afraid I'll need to sit to sew. I'll hurry." While she talked, she had been rummaging in a dresser drawer until she found the folded piece of green sateen left over from the blouse. I'd been saving this to make a dress for Betsy, she thought. I hope this doesn't ruin it.

"Let me hold the skirt up to you to see how long to make the ruffle," she said. "We'll get by without hemming it to save time. Maybe it'll do until your own clothes dry."

Without touching the woman's wet clothing, she gauged the distance from the hem to the floor. The skirt fell halfway between the knees and feet. "I think I'll just make a border on the bottom," she said. She clipped selvage on one side and tore the cloth. Sitting on her rocker, she stitched the material underneath the edge of the hem, gathering it a bit to make it fit.

"Ma'am," Mrs. Drumm said, "I don't know how to thank you for being so kind to me. I argued against Sid's determination to come here after what happened to our horses last fall. I hated everybody kin to your boy or them Sextons and vowed never to have any truck with y'all." She started to cry. "I held out as long as I could but, when the bridge washed out this morning, it hit our barn awhopping. It knocked out some of the boards in the wall. If it hadn't been for the loft floor holding it together, it would have fell in then and there. That frighted us that it might go ahead and fall in during the night and we'd lose our lives. We already lost nearly everything else."

Lillie had almost interrupted her when she mentioned the bridge. As soon as the woman stopped for breath, she said, "Are you talking about the bridge on the main road?"

"Yes'm. Sid said the supports must have give way and the whole thing crashed into the side of the barn before it broke apart. I mean, it made the loudest noise I ever heard and the whole building shook. It like to've scared the living daylights out of me."

"You were in the barn when it happened?"

"Oh, yes Ma'am. We ain't been able to stay in the house in over a week. The water riz in it right away. We moved into the barn so's we could take care of the horses and the cow and chickens. But today the cow and chickens washed away. The horses wandered off trying to find grass to eat and we don't know if we'll ever find them again. We ain't got nothing left."

Trying to soothe the woman, Lillie said in a cheerful tone, "You have your home and your farmstead."

Mrs. Drumm said, "No'm. We don't own the place. It belongs to some Indians that had so many children that they got two sections in the allotment. We rent on shares from them but we won't have any increase this year to pay the rent." She moaned and let her grief have full sway. By the time she got control of her emotions, Lillie had finished her alterations.

She wanted to put her arms around the distraught neighbor. Instead, she said, "You go behind the dresser and get out of those wet things and towel off. I'll hand you some underwear and these clothes to put on." Moving the porcelain wash basin from the dresser to the floor beside the privacy area formed by angling the bureau with its tall mirror across the corner, she said, "Just put your wet clothes in this."

She waited until she handed the underwear into the outstretched hand and said, "I'm going to see how Ida is coming with supper. You come on out when you're dressed."

Picking up the basin of wet towel and clothing, she made her way back into the front room. The men and boys had gathered around Sid Drumm as he told his story. Betsy snuggled in her father's lap, half-asleep.

Drumm told much the same tale as she had heard from his wife. Busying herself with wringing out the wet things, she almost blocked the sound of his voice until she heard him say, "We're moving on everwhen we can get out. As soon as the water goes down, I'll try to find my horses but I don't have much hopes. No telling what shape they'll be in; I dread it but I might have to shoot them."

Jed said, "Mr. Drumm, didn't you say that your barn has a good loft floor in it? I'd like to talk to you about getting hold of it if you have to tear the barn down."

Lillie remained mum but thought, I'm going to tell Matt that the barn may not belong to Drumm. According to his wife, he rents that place.

"Yes, that loft floor is the only thing that held the barn together. I don't know about tearing the barn down, though. I'm going to try to sell the place and the new owner might want the barn like it is."

Mrs. Drumm had come back into the room and heard the last words. Her face flushed and she ducked her head as she walked toward Lillie. "Tell me where to hang these clothes," she said. "Thank you for wringing them out."

Lillie grabbed a handful of the still-damp clothes they had hung behind the stove earlier in the day and pulled them down. "Right here," she said, trying to keep a civil tone of voice.

Drumm's voice cut through her words. "Yessir, like I said, 'We're moving on.' I'll try to sell my place before we go but, if I can't, I'll hire somebody to sell it for me. I've been thinking since you mentioned it, I'll go ahead and let you have the barn if you can use it. How much did you plan to pay?"

Lillie could contain no longer. "Matt," she said, "Will you carry Betsy to her bed and let her finish her nap?"

Ben jumped up and lifted Betsy from his father's arms. "I'll carry her," he said.

Spoken duplicity never came easily to Lillie even though she had silently deceived her family for several years right after Betsy's birth by not telling them that she no longer suffered spells of depression. Her voice shook as she said, "No, Ben. I need to talk to your Pa in private." The words sounded flat and harsh in her ears.

Mrs. Drumm looked her full in the face, her mouth contorting. She's scared to death of him, Lillie thought.

Matt must have heard desperation in her voice because he pushed out of his chair and took Betsy back without a word.

She heard Jed say, "I don't have anything but my saddle horse to trade unless we can work out something else."

Lillie almost ran to their room. Hearing her son's words, she knew she must stop any negotiations before they got out of hand. As soon as Matt laid Betsy on her bed, Lillie stood in front of him, arms akimbo. "That man is lying," she said. Her voice rose in pitch as the words tumbled out. "He doesn't own that place; his wife told me they are renters. I'd watch him like a hawk."

Matt nodded his head slowly while he absorbed her news. "I sensed something wrong, but I couldn't put my finger on it. He wouldn't look straight at me, kept shifting his eyes from one to the other of the boys and spinning his tales. They were hanging on every word. I thought he stretched it to make a good story but this goes beyond the pale. I'd kick them out if they had any place else to go."

"Where are we going to put them to sleep? We've used every inch of this house already."

Matt said, "I've been musing on that, but this revelation puts a whole new light on it. I'm afraid to trust him out of my sight. We'll put a bed up in the barn for Ben and Holt. I'll sleep with Drumm in the boy's bed and his wife can sleep with you in here."

As they returned to the front room, Matt asked, "How long is it till supper?"

Following his lead, Lillie replied as naturally as she could muster. "I'll check with Ida and let you know."

Ida heard her and said, "I'm just waiting to put the cornbread in."

"Wait until the men come back," Lillie told her. "They're going to put up a bed in the barn for the boys."

Matt said, "We'll carry the Drumm's sacks and hang up their things in the barn. Come on, boys."

Drumm made no offer to rise from his chair.

Matt said, his voice tight, "You need to go, too, Drumm. You can help us sort out the wettest things." It's his Texas Ranger voice, Lillie thought.

She watched them pick up the heavy sacks from the porch. Ben and Holt carried a stuffed cotton sack between them while the others each took a jam-packed pillowcase. Drumm loaded the loose things in his arms.

As soon as the men were out of earshot, Lillie confronted Mrs. Drumm. "I want to know the truth," she said. "Do you own the barn or anything else about the place?"

Mrs. Drumm looked about from one door to the other in the room, her eyes shifting back and forth like a trapped rat looking for a place to hide. Fear in her voice, she said, "It ain't none of it ourn." She sniffled as if trying not to cry. "I don't know what I'll do if you let on to Sid that I told you." As she talked, a trickle of snuff juice ran down each side of her mouth, staining it brown. She picked up the baking powder tin she used for a spit can and spat a stream into it.

Lillie turned her head away. I saw my Ma use snuff all my life, she thought, but she didn't make a mess with it. Even so, I vowed never to get started using the nasty stuff. I hope that woman doesn't stain everything she touches.

"I will tell no one but my husband," she said. "Whatever Matt does will be his decision, but I can see you're between a rock and a hard place and I'll explain that to him. He's a retired Texas Ranger, you know. He's handled all kinds of tricky situations in his time and he'll know what to do."

Mrs. Drumm let out her breath as if she had been holding it although she had been inhaling so shallowly that she had little air to exhale. Setting her spit can on the floor, she stood and started to the kitchen. "I'll help with supper," she said.

"No, no, you rest," Lillie hastened to say. "Ida is practicing putting together a meal all by herself. It'll be good training to have two more at table."

CHAPTER 7

Jed

Jed's excitement escalated as he carried the sack of items to the barn. If the timbers from the barn loft would be good enough to use to floor his cabin, he would have enough stone to make his fireplace. Especially if I can get that big rock out in one piece for the mantle, he thought.

Dropping back to walk beside Sid Drumm, he said, "Looks like the rain is stopping. See how light the sky is getting in the west? I think the sun will be out before this day is over. How long do you think it will be before we can go see about the barn?"

"I ain't ever seen a flood like this one so I don't have any idee. We'll just have to wait and see. In the meantime, I can look at your horse and see if he's worth trading for."

Jed felt his stomach knot and a queasiness rise to his throat. He gulped twice before he could answer Drumm. "He's five years old," he said. "I raised him from a colt and trained him myself. He's never been sick and he's sound as a dollar."

Matt had stopped to wait for the two of them to catch up. He fixed Drumm with a cold glare and said, "This boy is underage, Drumm. Any dealings you have with him, you talk to me."

That flew all over Jed. "Pa," he said, "I'm a married man with a baby to look out for. I can make my own deals. I have to do what's best for me and mine."

His Pa didn't back down. "The trade you and this man are figuring on is outside your authority. It must be done fair and legal and you won't be of legal age for more than a year. Any deal like this must meet with my approval."

Drumm protested. "It's not like a real estate deal where it has to be recorded at the courthouse. I've made trades like this all my life. I make my living swapping horses. Why, I've took everything under the sun in a trade. Yessiree."

Matt said, "Nevertheless, we'll say no more about it. Now, let's get on with the work we came out here to do."

Work of sorting and hanging Drumm's clothing and bedding on the lines they had strung across the barn required pulling down their own laundry. Finding most of it damp-dry, they piled it in a tub to take to the women to iron. Matt sent the boys to the loft to set up one of the iron bedsteads they had removed from the dugout. They lugged bedstead, springs, and mattress up the ladder tipping them over the edge of the loft floor and dragging them to a bare spot.

Ben said, "We'll have to bring some bedding from the house. I hope it's not too hot up here to sleep."

"It'll be fine," Jed said. "It's been cool for May." He couldn't keep his mind on the job and decided to leave the other boys to finish while he went back to stay with his Pa and Drumm. He wanted to hear every word of their conversation. Maybe he could keep Pa from interfering too much in his business. Pa has money in the bank and he doesn't understand the bind I'm in, he thought. I'll be switched if I get any more beholden to him than I already am. I want to get my family out of here and getting ahold of flooring will solve that problem.

As he jumped from the third rung of the ladder, he heard Matt say, "I plan to talk to Baxter Wilson before you talk any more deal with the boy. So you watch your tongue."

'The boy!' Jed fumed silently. When is he ever going to see me as a full-grown man? "I'm going back to the house," he said. "I'll take these clothes to Ma."

The sun peeked out briefly between broken clouds as he entered the kitchen door. He looked around for Vinnie and, not seeing her, went into their room. She lay on the bed beside a sleeping J. C.

"Why are you not out there helping with supper?" Jed accosted her.

"Lillie wanted Ida to do it all by herself. I offered to help but they shunted me to the side, as usual," she said.

Jed needed to fight with somebody. "Don't call my mother 'Lillie'," he said. "If you can't bring yourself to call her 'Mother Conover', you can at least refer to her as 'Mrs. Conover'."

For once Vinnie must not have wanted to fuss because she said, "I don't call her that to her face. What's got your dander up?"

Jed observed that their voices had risen with each exchange. He felt like yelling and screaming but they had to watch themselves in such close quarters. He reached for her hand and pulled her to her feet. Lifting J. C. to rest against his shoulder, he said, "The sun's out. Let's go for a walk before supper."

They headed up the slope toward the old track that led to the main road. "Drumm said the bridge washed out this morning," Jed said. "Let's see if we can get close enough to see how bad it is."

They found it slow going; Jed clutched J. C. against his chest with one arm as he helped Vinnie keep upright. After much slipping they reached a tree. Leaning against it, he said, "Maybe we'd better not try to go any farther."

Vinnie snuggled against him with the baby between them. "We're out of earshot now," she said. "Tell me what put the bee in your bonnet."

Jed's anger had smoldered just below the surface and quickly rose to strain his voice. "Pa's treating me like a little kid," he said. "I'm trying to make a deal with Drumm to trade for the loft floor in his barn and Pa is butting in and queering the deal. If I can get ahold of that lumber, I can put a floor in our house and we can go ahead and move in. I get so tired of having to watch every move I make and kowtowing to him all the time. I want us to get out on our own."

Vinnie nestled her head on his shoulder. "Me, too," she said. "We've been married almost eight months and never get to be by ourselves. Sometimes I think I can't take it anymore."

Jed bent to kiss her and J. C. woke up screaming. They burst out laughing. "Here, give him to me," Vinnie said. "He sounds like he's hungry."

"And wet," Jed said.

"He stays that way most of the time. It's so hard to keep diapers dry in this wretched weather. I hope this sun stays out and we get back to normal now."

After Vinnie fed J. C., they slipped and slid their way back to the house stopping to laugh at themselves every time they managed to keep from falling. This is the way marriage should be, Jed thought. We haven't had a chance to find this side of our relationship. Maybe we can make this thing work, after all. He pulled her to him just before they emerged from the woods. Then, taking J. C. from her and circling her with his other arm, they walked in step to the house.

They found all the others already seated at table. Ida's rolled out her lower lip in a pout. "It's about time you showed up," she said. "I was just fixing to ring the dinner bell."

Lillie cut in, "Ida has put on a good dinner. We'll wait while y'all get washed up."

When Vinnie caught a break in the polite dinner-table conversation, she said, "Mother Conover, I wonder if you have time to help me on my rug. I have all the material braided now but I don't know how to sew it together."

Ida's head jerked up. "We've got a number three wash tub of ironing and you want to know if Ma has time," she said.

Lillie said, "Now, Ida, we won't start the ironing until morning. We can work on the rug tonight."

"I'll help with the ironing," Vinnie said. "I'm a good hand to iron. I wish I had some sad irons of my own; then we could work a lot faster."

Mrs. Drumm spoke for the first time. "I won't try to dig my arns out of the mud if that's where they are. Something that heavy didn't wash away, I'll bet. I'm going to my daughter's and she has arns, anyway. I'll probably have to go Shank's Mare and I'll not walk and carry heavy sad arns. In fact, after we leave, you can have anything left in the house if you can clean it up."

Drumm's chatter had lasted the entire meal and he hurried to interrupt the women. "If I can find my animals, I have a mule and a draft horse. I think the cow and chickens are long gone. We'll load everything we can carry onto the animals but we'll have to hoof it ourselves."

"Where does your daughter live?" Matt asked.

"She ain't my daughter," Drumm said. "She was grown and married before me and the missus met. I don't know if she'll take us in or not. I don't care; I've never sponged off nobody."

You're doing it now, Jed thought. But who am I to talk? You can't help it anymore than I can. I vow never to get in this big a mess ever again. I swear I'll make it on my own, by hook or crook. I don't mean that; it's just a saying. I'll do things honest and fair; I'll work hard and we *will* make it.

True to Jed's prediction the sun shone the next day and it soon became evident that the rain had ended. High winds helped dry the ground as the water receded. Plez appeared a few days later with another boatload of provisions.

After the men carried the food from the boat, Lillie made a pot of coffee and they sat around the table drinking it and talking. Drumm chattered away as usual; Jed wished he'd just shut his mouth for once. Can't he see how much we'd like to visit, just us?

Matt said, "Plez, I thought I'd ask your Pa when I saw him but you may know. Who owns the property that Drumm lives on?"

Jed gasped. He couldn't believe that Pa, always the soul of courtesy, made such a remark while sitting at the table with a neighbor. But Jed could see that Matt's ploy had its desired effect; Drumm closed his lips tight.

"Why, yes, I do," Plez said, his face turning red as he looked at Drumm. "Didn't Mr. Drumm tell you? It belongs to my mother's cousin, Arch McIntosh. He lives a mile east on the next section."

Matt said, "Drumm tells me that the bridge knocked a hole in the barn and he thinks it's ruined. We'd like to see if the owner wants it torn down. We have some able-bodied men here who could handle that job for him and we'd do it for some of the salvage."

Jed looked at his father with more respect. That old man is pretty sharp, he thought. I don't know how he knew Drumm lied about owning the place but he sure kept me out of a pickle this time.

As soon as the water receded enough to pass over the road to Drumm's place, the men helped him carry all his belongings back. Matt had kept an eagle eye on him at all times and made certain that he took no more than his own things. They found the buildings in a sorry mess: knee-deep mud in the barn and water still surrounding the dwelling a depth of six inches. Indeed the hole in the side of the barn caused by the bridge collision had rendered the barn unusable and, Jed thought, unfixable. He felt sorry for Mrs. Drumm but not for Sid. I never could stand a liar, he thought.

"We'll bring over a ladder," Matt said, "so you can climb up to the loft. We'll need it, anyway, if McIntosh lets us tear the barn down."

On the way home, Jed said to his father, "I can nail up a quick ladder from scraps so he won't get much if he absconds with it. I don't trust him any further than I can throw a bull by his tail. It'll take a couple of good two-bys for the stiles but we can more than replace them if we get to tear that barn down."

Arch McIntosh seemed happy to have the offer Matt and Jed put to him. "Tear the barn and house both down," he said. "All those buildings were built too close to the creek in the first place. If you trust me for it, we can deal on the lumber for the house after you get it stacked. My boys are getting big enough that we can handle both places now. I don't intend to rebuild right away but it won't hurt to have some lumber on hand."

Matt extended his right hand. "I've found every McIntosh that I've had any dealings with to be open and above-board. And, of course, Plez is my own son-in-law. So I have more than one reason to trust you."

Pa sure knows how to make a deal, Jed thought. I can learn a lot from the old man. He and Ben shook hands with McIntosh. Holt fell in behind Ben and struck hands, too. Jed had a hard time keeping his inward smile from touching his lips. He thinks he's a man now, he thought. We'll see if he can handle a man's work.

By the time the water receded enough for them to start working, the Drumm couple were long gone. McIntosh told Jed that they left owing him money but he'd rather have that nuisance out of his hair. No one seemed to know whether they found any of their animals but they took too much stuff with them to carry it on foot. Drumm had beaten the rails off the stiles of the ladder and the two-bys were gone. About as I expected, Jed thought; he didn't get much.

All the cotton crop next to the creek had washed away. A scraggly remnant of the upland field remained and his father decided to leave it and concentrate on replanting the washed-out field. While they waited for the land to dry enough to plow, all the men worked on tearing down the McIntosh buildings. They stacked the loft floor on Ben's wagon as they tore it down and Jed and Ben drove it across the road to Matt's place using a team of mules that McIntosh let them borrow, stacking it close to the creek as near Jed's house as they could.

"I wish we had a way through these woods for the wagon," Ben said. "The creek is narrow right here so we can carry it across when the ground dries up enough."

When Ben, Holt and Jed began to demolish the dwelling, Jed found a stone fireplace on the far side that he had not seen before. Excitement filled him as he went inside and saw the mantle cut from one stone that he judged to be six feet long. It's not as big as the one buried in Ben's hillside, he thought, but it would sure be easier to get if I can figure out a way to transport it to the site. He examined the other components of the fireplace and found them to be of less quality than he had envisioned for his own construction. Most of them would not please him for show. But there'll be plenty material needed inside the chimney, he thought. And somehow I'll have to figure out how to make the mortar.

Hurrying outside, he told Ben, "I want to see what Pa thinks about me trying to make a deal for the fireplace. I'm going home right now and talk to him. I hope his rheumatism has let up so he feels like coming back with me to look this over and then going to see McIntosh."

Ben laughed. "Johnny-jump-up," he said. "Can't you wait until dinner?"

Jed laughed with him. Then he turned serious. "You don't know how much I want to get out on my own," he said. "I'd like to tie it down on the fireplace. We could move in as soon as I get the floor finished and then I'll be at home so I can work on the rest of the house better. Vinnie can cook in the yard during the summer and fall but we have to have heat inside before winter."

Ben winked at Holt. "Go on, then," he said to Jed. "Leave us to carry the load alone."

As Jed walked away from them, he worried, I don't know what I'll use to trade. I don't have two cents to rub together.

McIntosh proved to be a good neighbor. "If you'll fix the cattle pens and show my boys how to build a little barn and sheds, we'll call it even for the stone. I'll loan you my mules again to move them. But I suggest you wait until the road is fixed and carry them around the section line."

"I don't know how long it will be before they get around to the road," Jed said. "I need the fireplace built before winter."

"I heard that the road crews will be out in our part of the county later this summer," McIntosh said. "You might could check at the store and see if Baxter knows. You can leave the rock here as long as you need to."

As they returned home, Jed told his Pa, "I'm going to see Mr. Wilson today, if you don't need me. I need to make some money, too, so I'll ask him to put in a good word for me and see if I can go to work for the county on the road."

SUMMER 1908

CHAPTER 8

Ben

Ben rose before dawn the morning of Saturday, July 4, 1908 and hurried through his chores. The citizens of Chagris had decided to hold a big celebration to observe the first year the new state had a chance to honor the nation's birthday. Mr. Wilson explained that the town's merchants intended to make the observance an annual affair and decided it must start the first year. In addition to providing a vacant block for the picnic grounds and building the platforms and tables, they had solicited watermelons from area farmers and had them cooling in the ice dock planning to serve them in late afternoon.

Ben intended to ride his horse to the picnic so he could arrive long before his Pa's slower wagon transported the rest of the family. If this celebration turned out to be anything like similar ones he had attended in Texas, he expected to enter his horse in a race and also to try to sign up for a place on one of the baseball teams. He looked forward to a day filled with food, contests, and political speeches. Eligible to vote for the first time, he wanted to hear all the arguments from every candidate. He and Pa had already engaged in a little sparring because Pa couldn't see for the life of him why anyone would vote anything but a straight Democrat ticket. Of course, a man had to register Democrat to vote in the county elections, but Ben figured on keeping an open mind and vote for the man, not the party. Although the Democrat party convention wasn't scheduled until later in the month, the Republicans had already picked William Howard Taft to head their ticket. Perhaps some representative of that party would speak on his behalf.

Jed wanted to ride in with him, but when he mentioned it to Vinnie, she threw such a fit that he had given up and made arrangements to come with his parents. Ben suspected that Jed didn't mind as much as he let on because he wanted to show off his son. I've never seen anyone as foolish about a baby as Jed turned out to be, he thought. He had to admit his own fondness for the little nipper himself although he couldn't figure out why. He wouldn't tell Jed, but he thought the baby the ugliest infant he ever did see, looking like a miniature Hiram Wade. No part of him resembled a Conover. Maybe he would grow out it; Ben hoped so.

Anxious to get to the rally but not wanting to tire his horse out, he alternated between an easy trot and a walk. As he neared the McMasters place, he pulled his mount to a slow walk hoping to catch a glimpse of Esther. He had given up and had put his horse into a trot again when Holt caught up with him.

"Ma let me borrow her little mare," he said. "Ida wanted to ride her but I begged Ma into letting me have her instead. Ida's spittin' mad because the horses are too big for her. She hates to listen to Vinnie all the way to town but I reckon it's better her than me."

Ben chuckled. He felt the same way about Vinnie but felt sorry for her, too. Her Pa had treated her like dirt and he thought his family should be kinder to her. Vowing to be nicer to her in the future, he put her out of his mind and looked forward to the holiday.

Once at the fairgrounds, he saw that the McMasters boys had already arrived and were sitting on the makeshift stage tuning their instruments. Townspeople in charge of this year's celebration had gone all out with their preparations. The speaker's platform, draped in red, white and blue bunting, had been erected under a large tree. They had arranged to have a well-known judge from a neighboring county deliver the key oration before the noon meal. Ben expected a stirring message about the role of Oklahoma as the newest star in the greatest nation on earth. After lunch any man who planned to run in the county primary scheduled for later in the summer would be given a chance to make his case. The speakers could expect shade from the spreading branches overhead to alleviate somewhat the warmth of their wool suits and high collared shirts. Fortunately, Ben thought, nobody expected farmers to dress up quite so much.

The stage where the McMasters men sat enjoyed less shade. Built next to a small dance floor, it boasted a piano and set of drums as well as a number of chairs for the performers. Someone had scythed the large grassy area around the stage and dance floor to provide ample room for square dancers. To one side, tables made from two-by-twelves fastened together with cleats and resting on barrels already held a smattering of the abundant food that would grace them by noon.

Ben spied Esther and her mother setting out bowls and pans and covering them with colorful cloths to protect the food from flies. He didn't approach them but looked around for the place to register for the horse races and for baseball. Holt had found some school chums and joined a game of pitching washers.

The Wilsons arrived and parked their buggy near the tables. Plez jumped out and tethered the horse while his father helped Flora and Polly out. Flora wore a loose fitting dress that disguised her pregnancy well. Ben knew that she would not appear in public again until after the baby's birth except for attending worship services. He hoped to help make this day special for her.

After he and his father unloaded baskets of food for the picnic, Plez moved the buggy, unhitched his horse and settled him in the roped-off space that served as a temporary corral.

Ben joined him. "Morning, Brother," he said. "You're just the fellow I want to see. I found the place to sign up for the horse races but I want to find a ball team, too, if I can."

"Our team is made up of Indians," Plez said, "but the town team is always looking for good players. Here, I'll take you to find some of their bunch."

The local team seemed glad to find a shortstop but asked Ben if he could also pitch in case they had trouble finding enough players. He agreed to return shortly after lunch to play in the game scheduled before the afternoon speaking. After he shook hands to seal the bargain, he and Plez found a shady spot to stand while they listened to the featured speaker.

The mayor and other city fathers rose from their chairs to shake hands with a newcomer and led him to the seat of honor. The town band immediately struck up a medley of lively tunes beginning with *Columbia, the Gem of the Ocean* and switching to *When Johnny Comes Marching Home*. By the time they had progressed to the newer songs—*America the Beautiful* and *You're a Grand Old Flag*—most of the men had gathered around the dais. As the band launched into the state song of the new state, Everett McMasters led the assembled throng in singing the words. His clear baritone carried the verse almost by itself, but the crowd chimed in on the chorus and finished with a rousing cheer.

Known for his great oratory, the judge had been the first choice of the program committee. Even as a young defense attorney, he had seldom lost a case. In the first election of the new state, he had won by a landslide. When he rose to speak, his presence commanded attention and the hubbub ceased.

Ben listened as the man spoke first of the birth of the nation, the wisdom of those first planners of the constitution, and the history of the last one hundred thirty-two years. When he extolled the bravery of soldiers in the great conflict that divided our nation, Ben saw several old men stand a little straighter. Ben's heart swelled with pride as he remembered his Grandfather Holt. Even though he had died when Ben was a lad, he had paraded in his uniform for his small grandsons and they had marched behind shouldering their wooden rifles.

As the judge rounded out his speech, he turned to the significance of the forty-sixth star in the nation's flag. The "land of sun and flowers" had such great potential, he said, and needed men of honor and integrity to raise its corn and cotton, to instill great principles in its children, and to consider filling the offices of the cities, county, and state.

For the first time since Ben left his beloved Texas, he felt a pull to be a part of this new land. He had heard his mother call it a raw, red land and had concurred in her description. But the orator had persuaded him that a young man had opportunities in this young state that were unavailable to him elsewhere. During the months since Paul's death, Buford's departure, and even after Jed's return, he had felt compelled to stay and help out on the farm. Though he did his best to hide his reluctance, he had never been able to give his whole heart to his new situation. Even when he bought his acreage he harbored the thought that he could sell it when he went back home. Esther McMasters had exerted the one tug on his heart that made him want to stay. As the speech ended, he made up his mind to start courting Esther in earnest and to put the pull of Texas behind him.

The speech ended to sustained applause and shouts of approval. The master of ceremonies urged everyone to enjoy their dinner and reconvene after the ballgame to hear the slate of candidates. Plez tapped Ben's arm. "Let's go find Flossie. She wants to get Esther to spread her lunch with us and told me to bring you along."

Ben decided that arrangement suited him just fine. It would give him an opportunity to talk to Esther without putting any pressure on her. He would try his best to hide his feelings and just have fun.

Flora sent Plez to get a quilt from the buggy to use as a tablecloth. She and Esther had picked a good flat spot under a shade tree and had left Betsy to hold it for them until they could get the quilt spread. "I think that little feisty thing can hold her own with anybody who might try to take it away from her," Flora said with a laugh. She pointed toward their little sister standing stolidly looking up at a couple of tall girls and gesturing with both arms.

"I'll go help her," Ben said. "Is she going to eat with us?"

"No. I promised her a pulley bone for holding the spot and I made arrangements with Ma to be sure Betsy eats with them. I thought I'd have more trouble with Ida and Polly but they seem to have found a big gang of boys and girls their age. They're ignoring old married folks like Plez and me."

"Flossie, are you playing matchmaker?" Ben asked. "Because it might put Esther in an awkward position."

A smile played around Flora's lips but she quickly turned serious. "It's time she started to get over Jed. She'll never find anyone better than you. I know how you feel about her."

Annoyed, Ben said, "Don't push it, Sis. Let's just have a good time today and let it go at that."

Plez returned with the quilt and he and Ben took it to the chosen spot. Taking Betsy by the hand, Ben said, "Come on, Punkin, let's go find Ma and get ready for the blessing."

Once they had filled their plates they returned to their picnic location. Flora had Ben carry Plez's plate so that he had both hands to carry a basket. "I brought a second peach cobbler for us," she said.

Ben felt a little uncomfortable knowing Flora's purpose in arranging the foursome but Esther said, "Didn't Judge What's-his-name give a stirring lecture?"

The others burst into laughter. Plez teased, "Are you going to quote him to anybody? Maybe you'd better learn his name."

Esther tried to frown at them but couldn't stop a giggle. "You all know how I am about names," she said. "Just overlook it." Her expression turned serious again. "I've lived in Indian Territory most of my life," she continued, "without thinking about it one way or the other. He made me proud to be an Oklahoman."

Ben said, "You know, Old What's-his-name made me feel like I have a chance to grow with this new state. I think I'll stay."

Flora stared at him in surprise. "I didn't know you had any other plans," she said. "I know you wanted to go back to Texas when you first came, but after you bought that land and all I thought you'd changed your mind."

"No. I felt two ways about it. I bought that land for an investment. I thought I could always sell it if I went back. But I made up my mind today. I'm not going back."

Flora put her hand on his. "Ben, I'm glad. You'll settle down here and have a family and our children can grow up together."

Ben's eyes signaled her to watch it even as he chuckled. "You've got my future all planned, haven't you? Maybe I have something to say about that."

They finished their meal and Plez lay back and put his arms under his head. Flora leaned down and whispered in his ear. He pushed himself up and took her hand. "Will y'all excuse us?" he said. "We'll be back in a little bit." They walked side by side to the far side of the picnic grounds.

Esther's face and neck turned beet red. She jumped up, turned as if to run and stepped on the hem of her dress. In order to keep her from falling, Ben made a grab for her and caught her foot. She looked down, lost her tenuous balance and fell headlong into the leftover food.

"Oh," she wailed. "Oh, *look* what I've *done*."

Ben helped her to a sitting position. Squashed tomatoes and little kernels of corn mingled with potato salad and peach cobbler stuck to the front of her dress.

"Oh, dear, oh, dear," Esther said. "I can't let anybody see me like this. I'll have to go home. But I can't go home. Pa made arrangements for us to sing at the entertainment after the ball game. Oh-h, what *will* I do?"

Ben cast about in his mind for some way to keep her at the picnic. "You just sit here," he said. "I'll go find Flossie and we'll come up with something. We'll find some way so you can stay and enjoy the rest of the day."

He left before she could demur. Meeting Plez and Flora on their way back, he explained the situation.

Flora immediately took charge. "Get me a pan of water," she said to Plez. "We need to get the food sponged off her dress before it ruins it."

When she saw the state of the damage, she decided that they needed more privacy. "Bring our buggy to the roadside next to us," she said. "We'll get in it so no one can see me scrub her down."

Suddenly, the situation became hilarious to everyone but Esther. Miffed at their uncontrolled laughter, she burst into tears. Ben sobered. In all his life he had never wanted to put his arms around anyone so much. He looked icicles at the Wilsons.

"Come on, Esther," he said. "Go with Flossie. She'll get you fixed up in no time."

Esther tried to feel in her pocket for a handkerchief and encountered food. She held up her hand and looked at it as if she had never seen it before. She began to giggle and glanced covertly at Flora who hooted with laughter.

"You are an unholy mess," Flora said when she could get her breath.

"I guess I might as well laugh as cry," Esther said. "Do you think we really can clean me up enough so that I can appear on stage?"

"We can try. Come on."

They were gone so long that Ben worried the sponging process hadn't worked. When Flora pushed aside the buggy curtains and descended alone, his anxiety threatened to overwhelm him. "Didn't it work?" he asked.

"It took a lot of scrubbing," Flora said. "Now she is sopping wet and afraid it won't dry in time. I can't get her to come out. Go talk to her."

"You could get her to go for a walk and find a sunny spot out of sight where she could lie in the sun until the dress dried," he told Flora.

"That sounds like a good idea, Ben, but I can't do it. I promised Plez I'd watch the ballgame and bring refreshments to his team afterward. He's already gone over to the ball ground. You could take her. Take the quilt for her to lie down on."

"Flossie, you know I can't do that. It would ruin her reputation."

"I guess it would at that. Well, I know you'll think of something." Flora turned and hurried away leaving him standing there wondering what to say to convince Esther to come out of the buggy.

He looked around. All the picnickers had moved to the other side of the block where the afternoon's activities were scheduled. Women worked at the serving tables packing food for transport home but no one seemed to be paying any attention to them. He went to the buggy.

"Esther," he said, "Everyone's gone off and left us alone here. I have an idea. Come go with me for a walk and let your dress dry. It's a hot day and it shouldn't take very long. Come on, it'll never dry in there."

"All right. I don't see what else I can do," she agreed. "Please go tell Ma what has happened and have her send me my parasol so I won't sunburn."

They walked slowly down the road away from town with neither of them speaking for a time. Esther broke the silence. "I'm so embarrassed. I've taken you away from all the good times you looked forward to today."

Ben broke in. "I'd rather be with you. That's the best time I could have."

She turned to look at him with a startled expression. Uh-oh, he thought, I'm going a little fast for her. She bowed her head and stared at the ground. A tear brimmed over and trickled down her cheek unchecked.

"I'm sorry," he said. "I didn't mean to make you cry but you can't help knowing how I feel about you."

"Ben, you're such a good man…."

"But?"

"But I'm not ready to talk to any man right now. It's been such a trying day and, *look* at me. My dress is still wet and I know my nose and eyes are red and no telling what my hair looks like."

You look beautiful to me, he thought. "When we go back to the shindig after your dress dries, we'll laugh at this fiasco. I know you don't believe it now, but you wait and see. This day will turn out fine. I think what we need to do right now, though, is to find someplace you can face the sun until your dress dries. We're not too far from the church. You might could lean against a west wall or something."

"I guess that's the best we can do. But look at the edges where it's beginning to dry. They are so wrinkled I'd be ashamed to appear in public let alone sing on the stage." Her tearful voice threatened another outburst. Ben tried desperately to think of something to distract her.

"I wonder what happened to the Goodgions," he said. "Did you see anything of them today?"

"I saw the boys and their families," she said, "but not Brother or Sister Goodgion. We need to check on them. Would you do that while I try to bake this dress in the sun?"

He stole a glance at her without turning his head. She had regained her sense of humor. He liked that about her; she could laugh at herself. Too, she seemed to be able to change to a better mood by taking charge.

At the meetinghouse, they found that the steps to the side door offered a seat in a good slice of sunlight. Esther positioned herself so that the patch of brightness fell on her wet clothing. She leaned back until her head and hands found shade from the overhanging eaves.

Expecting the sun to dry her dress in a short while, Ben went next door to inquire about the parson and his wife. Mr. Goodgion came to the door and assured him that they were well but had decided against attending the function because of their duties on the morrow.

"I've recovered from my sick spell," he said. "I need to study my sermon more today and Mrs. Goodgion plans to invite company for dinner. At our age it takes longer to prepare, you know. So what brings you away from the celebration? Not just to check on us, I hope."

Mrs. Goodgion appeared in the doorway to the kitchen, wiping her hands on her apron.

While he shook hands with her, Ben explained Esther's plight.

"We can take care of that right away," Mrs. Goodgion said. "I've got the stove hot cooking for tomorrow. I'll put the iron on. You go get Esther and we'll iron that dress dry."

Esther sprang up from her perch when Ben delivered Mrs. Goodgion's invitation. "That sounds like the best idea I've heard today," she said. "I wonder what she's got for me to wear while we iron it." She giggled.

Ben loved the sound of her delighted titter. Considering the size of the preacher's wife compared to tiny Esther, he guffawed. "Whatever it is, she'll have to wrap it around you three times."

"Now you men stay out here on the porch until we get our business attended to," Mrs. Goodgion told them. "Mr. Goodgion, would you mind drawing us all a cool drink? I'm sure these young people would enjoy that."

"I'll do it, Mr. Goodgion," Ben said. "Just show me where."

Settled in the porch chairs with a pitcher of fresh cool well water between them, the men rocked and sipped the water. "I don't want to keep you from your study," Ben said. "I'll be fine here. You go on about your business."

"You heard me get my orders," the preacher said. "I learned long ago that when the missus has a bee in her bonnet, I'd better follow orders."

Ben felt more comfortable than he had expected. He chuckled. "I know it's that way around our house, but I thought a preacher, of all men, would run things."

"That's the way it is around any man's house. Take my advice, Ben. When you marry you wear the britches but she washes and irons them. Remember that."

"I'll try to," Ben said.

"Maybe it's none of my business but I like to know what's going on with my flock. I'm not surprised to see you and Esther together, but it's the first time, isn't it?"

"Yes, it is." Ben took another sip of water. "Mr. Goodgion, I feel like I can trust you to keep a confidence. If I have my way, it won't be the last time.

Esther, on the other hand, has no such feelings for me. So, for the time being we will just have to let things go on the way they have been."

"You can trust me. From what I've seen of you, she could do worse. As faithful as Esther is, I'm surprised that I haven't seen you at services."

"Yes, well…" Ben didn't know what to say.

"I don't mean to push you. I meant to say that you'd always be welcome."

Esther pushed the door open and strode onto the porch. She looked beautiful to Ben with her dress freshly pressed and hair combed and pinned in a smooth knot at the back of her neck. No longer did her eyes and nose look red, either. All the events of the day might never have happened.

"Mr. Goodgion," he said, "I thank you for your hospitality and you and your good wife for all your help. I wonder if I could impose on you to wash up and comb my hair." He winked at Esther and she dimpled. This day is turning out better than we hoped, he thought.

"I wonder what time it is," Esther said on the way back. "Do you think I'll be in time for my family's appearance on the program? Should we hurry?"

"Well, I don't think we should run. It wouldn't be dignified."

Esther giggled and drew herself up to her full diminutive height. "We must be dignified at all costs. Pshaw, I'd rather just have fun."

"We'll have fun. I wish I could ask you to stay for the dancing later, but I don't know how I'd get you home. I rode my horse. I could walk and lead him but it's too far to your place to walk."

"My brothers will be playing for the dancing. I can go home with them. I'd be honored to have you for a partner in the square dancing."

Esther went to find her father and Ben walked over to the diamond. He found the ballgame in the bottom half of the ninth inning with the town team behind four runs. Ben watched Plez pitch a fast ball that just caught the corner of the strike zone for the last out.

The captain of the town team stomped over to Ben. He's madder than a wet hen, Ben thought. I don't blame him.

"You're a little late for the game," the captain said. "What happened to you?"

"Something came up and I didn't have time to let you know. Didn't Plez tell you?"

"Yeah, he said you had to take your sweetheart for a walk. Couldn't wait till after dark, huh?"

Ben hit him.

By the time Plez pulled them apart Ben's shirt sported blood and his knuckles smarted from the blows. He shook the hair out of his eyes and fixed his opponent with a steady glare. The man's nose spouted blood and one eye didn't open. "Don't you ever say such a thing again or I'll do worse than bloody your nose," Ben said.

The captain wiped his nose on his sleeve and studied the crowd of men that ringed them. "I'm sorry," he said. "I don't know anything about you and I don't even know who the girl is. I'm spitting mad that we lost the game playing with a man short but I shouldn't have let my mouth run off." He rubbed his hand on his pants leg and offered it to Ben.

Ben hesitated and had to force himself to shake it. "If we ever get another chance to play ball, I'll do my best to be on time," he said. "That is, if you still want me."

"We're always looking for good players. Let me change that; we're looking for any kind of player. Are you any good?"

"Back home our county team won every game last season. I'll let that record speak for itself."

Plez interrupted. "You boys had better go get cleaned up. The afternoon program is about to start."

Flora teased him as she sponged the blood from his shirt. "Looks like you and Esther are determined to get your clothes dirty today. You remind me of two little kids."

"At least, it's not my blood. The other fellow got the worst of this encounter." Ben washed his face and hands and combed his hair and managed to take his place in the audience just before the McMasters quartet accompanied by Claude, Arnold, and Beulah began their song. It may be my imagination, he thought, but I think Esther knew when I showed up. She didn't nod at me but she smiled; she must have been watching for me. His heart leaped at the slight encouragement.

While the candidates spoke, the ladies cut and sliced the cold watermelons furnished by the farmers. No representatives of national candidates appeared and that disappointed Ben. Determined to weigh all the arguments on both sides before marking his ballot, he meant to make his first time to vote count.

Several of the families in their neighborhood gathered together to eat their watermelon and he and Plez joined them. The older couples decided to go on home to take care of their chores while leaving the young people to enjoy the evening festivities. McMasters took Beulah with them while Ben's folks made Holt and Betsy go with them. Holt put up a fuss. He's beginning to think he's grown, Ben thought.

"I'm going to rest a while and let my melon settle," Plez said. "Then I want to challenge Ben and his partner to a game of horseshoes. Who wants to be my partner, ladies?"

No one volunteered right away. Ben laughed. "I'll see if I do any better than you, Plez. Will you be my partner, Esther?" He expected her to be shy but she seemed eager to join him as his partner. Plez chose Polly and the foursome moved to the improvised court accompanied by their friends who chose a team to support and stationed themselves on opposite sides of the court. Both men stepped off ten feet in front of their chosen stake for the ladies' pitching positions. Several pairs of horseshoes offered a choice of weights. The players tried them for heft and feel and made a selection.

"Ladies first," Plez said.

"Okay," Polly agreed, "but we switch on opposite rounds."

Both her horseshoes went wild. "I'll have to get the swing of it," she said. Her brother made an elaborate show of trying to hide his snicker. "We'll see who gets the last laugh," she told him. "Remember I've got a partner."

Esther stepped forward to the line and adjusted her skirt to fall smoothly around her ankles. Holding her first horseshoe on the shank near the heel caulk, she sighted it and brought it back. Just before she reached her full back swing, she stepped forward with her left foot and, as she swung the shoe even with that foot, straightened her bent knees and released the shoe at eye level. The wobbling shoe arced and settled on the stake, a dead ringer.

Shouting and clapping, her fans rooted so loudly that a crowd began to gather. Her next shot landed to the left of the stake not quite touching her ringer. She smiled and walked back out of Plez' way.

He took his stance and, with no wasted motions placed his first shoe around the post canceling her ringer. Boos erupted from Esther's gallery but he ignored them. Taking a little more time to line up with the target, he released the shoe and followed through as metal clanged on metal totaling six points. Plez swept off his hat and bowed deeply to Esther's rooters while his supporters shouted and whistled.

The two teams were well matched. Plez shone at the game while Polly settled into her game making a few points. Ben and Esther were both good players. The match seesawed back and forth until, as they neared the agreed upon final score, one point separated them. Plez and Polly needed three points and Ben and Esther had to make four.

The men pitched first. Ben scored a leaner. Plez' first shoe ringed the post completing their necessary points and his second leaned at a wide angle. Polly flung both tries wide of the mark.

Esther took her time getting set. Carefully she lined up her shot and flicked it into the air. It went high sailing over the pin and landing two feet behind it. A concerted groan went up from her fans. She took half a step to the left and went through her routine again without the shoe. Then she grasped the shoe firmly, sighted, brought her arm back in one smooth motion, stepped forward with her left foot and shifted her weight as she delivered the pitch with a delicate wrist-motion. The horseshoe moved lazily through the air, turned just as it crossed the foul line and circled the stake canceling Plez' ringer as it hit his leaner with a clang and sent it hurtling out of the field of play. Esther dusted her hands together and grinned at Plez.

Silence reigned in both galleries for a moment as the spectators watched in disbelief. Then her enthusiasts shouted and whistled and thronged her with congratulations, the girls hugging her and the men shaking her hand. The other side joined in the applause.

Ben watched Plez gather the horseshoes from his end of the court. Picking up the four near him, he met his brother-in-law half way. Extending his hand, he said, "Good match. I wish I played half as well as you do."

Plez chuckled and shook his head. "Beaten by a slip of a girl," he said. "I'll never live this down."

The balance of the events of the day only served to heighten Ben's spirits. Esther seemed content to be with him and to cheer at the finish line as he won the horse race. Before the dancing started in late afternoon, his family and the McMasters clan spread their supper together. Cold fried chicken and hunks of homemade bread, sliced tomatoes, cold corn on the cob, and several varieties of pickles made up a hearty meal. Flora brought out two apple pies she had left in their buggy, cut them into fourths, and handed them around.

"I'm too full to dance," Ben said.

"Don't worry," Claude told him. "I have to let my supper settle before I can play a note."

As the sun settled low, the McMasters ensemble started playing a lively tune and the young people assembled from all sections of the block. As soon as a sufficient number gathered, Claude rose, tucked his fiddle under his chin and played a riffle. "Choose your partners for a square," he said and launched into a hoedown.

Ben bowed to Esther, extended his hand and asked her, "Will you join me?"

She giggled and walked beside him to a place in one of the quadrilles. Ida and one of the town youths positioned themselves on his right as Claude began calling the steps. Ben had always enjoyed square dancing but he felt he had never stepped so lightly as he did that night with Esther keeping step beside him as they held hands crossed in front of them. When Claude concluded the dance with "Promenade right off the floor", he escorted her to get a drink of water.

"Ben, I enjoyed that," she said.

"See, I told you. This day has turned out fine."

They heard the band start playing a waltz and, knowing that Esther sat out the round dances, he found them a place on one of the benches scattered throughout the park. They sat in a companionable silence listening to the music. At the end of the waltz, they heard the bouncy rhythm of a schottische.

"Esther," Ben said, "I expect them to call another square dance next. Before we go back, I want to ask you something."

He felt rather than saw her tension but she said nothing.

"I'd like permission to call on you."

She took her time in replying. He felt the humidity of the sultry air and heard the beat of the music and of his own heart as he inhaled and exhaled several shallow breaths. It seemed like an eternity to him before she said a word.

Not looking at him, she said, "I told you this afternoon that I'm not ready to talk to any man. I've had a good time and enjoyed your company today." She turned to face him. "Can't we just leave it at that?"

"If that's the way it must be, I guess I can accept that answer for now," he said. "But it's not what I want to hear. And it won't be the last time I'll ask you. I'll try not to make a nuisance of myself, of course, but I hope it won't be too long before you change your mind."

CHAPTER 9

Esther

Esther spent a restless night. Sleep eluded her for hours, it seemed, while she relived the problems of the day, running them over and over through her mind. She tried to think only of the fun and triumphs but the memory of Ben's voice saying 'it won't be the last time I'll ask you' insisted on intruding. She knew that she'd have to face a final decision some day but she didn't want to think about that now.

Troubled dreams disturbed her slumber when she did drift off. She again wore the food-encrusted dress as Jed looked at her in disgust. Behind him holding a cat wrapped in a quilt from Esther's hope chest Vinnie stood laughing at her. Jed tried to wipe the food off her dress but the food came off in chunks making holes in the dress. As she watched in horror, the dress started melting like an icicle in the sun until she stood on the stage in a tattered dress singing a hymn. She tried to cover her exposure or turn away but found no hiding place.

Awakened rudely by a rough shake from Beulah, she sat up in bed and looked at her surroundings. The vivid dream slowly receded.

"You were thrashing around and woke me up," her sister said, sounding like a cross baby. "You must have been having a nightmare."

"I guess so," Esther said. "I'm glad you woke me."

She lay back in bed for what seemed an interminable length of time while Beulah's steady inhaling and exhaling grated on her nerves until she could stand it no longer. Bounding from the bed, she ran out into the night not bothering to take her shoes. She paced the hard-packed yard for a few minutes and then headed for the clearing as if pulled on a string. Many times in the months since Jed had married Vinnie, she had gone there to replay in her memory scene after scene of their courtship. She always ended up crying and had to stop by one of the stock ponds to wash her face before going home.

Determined to put the past behind her, she told herself that this one last visit would be her way of saying goodbye to girlish fantasies and might-have-beens. Picking her way through the underbrush in the dark almost deterred her but she pressed on. Branches caught at her thin gown and once a goathead thorn pierced her foot. Crying with pain as she rested the foot against the opposite knee and tried easing the thorn out, she considered turning back. Her eyes had grown accustomed to the dark by then and she could see the clearing a few feet ahead. Jerking the thorn out, she threw it as far as she could send it and pushed her way through the remaining undergrowth.

Once in the clearing, she wended her way from tree to tree on its outer rim running her hand along each trunk. Talking to the trees as if they could hear her, she told each one of them goodbye. Then she stood in the middle of the small space and raised her head to look at the sky. She remembered it in moonlight and in full daylight, in starshine and in darkness. This night seemed darker than at any time before but she thought it might be her imagination. "I won't be back," she said. "I'm through with wallowing in my own pity; I'm going to make a life for myself."

In her mind, she heard Ben ask her if he could call on her and she answered aloud, "Not yet, Ben. First I'm going to find out who I am without Jed or you or anybody else."

She stayed until the first fingers of day touched the eastern sky. Taking a more circuitous route she soon reached a cow path and followed it home. Standing on the back porch, she poured water into the wash pan and washed her feet before returning to bed. Beulah stirred as she slipped in beside her but didn't waken.

Esther must have drifted right off because her mother's wake-up call startled her out of a sound sleep. "I thought I'd let you girls sleep late this morning," Judith said. "You had a busy day yesterday."

The week went better than Esther expected. At church that morning some of the girls teased her about Ben but she knew that they approved. Prudence Goodgion hugged her and whispered that she looked beautiful. Canning chores kept her and her mother busy all week along with the ordinary work required by a household of seven. Beulah helped a little bit but sometimes her constant chatter got on Esther's nerves. But neither did she want to think too much about the decision she had made Saturday night to make a new life for herself. She wanted the moves she made to be the right ones and didn't intend to let her innate impatience overcome her good sense.

The nights proved the hardest challenge but Polly Wilson had loaned her a copy of Gene Stratton-Porter's *Freckles*. She read by kerosene lamp light in the kitchen until her eyelids drooped. Sleep came easily then.

The following Sunday morning her father called her to the front room privately. "Esther, we need to talk about something your brothers told me." He cleared his throat as if the words stuck in it. "Claude and Horace played last night at a dance in town; you know, the kind I would like them to turn down. They're grown men, though. But that's off the subject. More to the point, they overheard a group of men talking and it appears your reputation is being bandied about in those low circles."

Esther's heart sank. "Pa," she said, "I've never done anything wrong in my whole life as far as I know."

"You know you must avoid the very appearance of evil. At any rate, Claude questioned until he got to the root of it. This man that Ben had the fight with at the picnic has spread all kinds of rumors and told it for fact. Your walking off from the picnic with Ben seems to be the basis for the gossip."

"But, Pa, we walked straight to Preacher Goodgion's. Sister Goodgion helped me clean up my clothes and we came right back."

"Daughter, you know the old saying that gossip is like feathers. When it's let loose on the wind, there's no calling it back. What we must do is figure out what measures to take to keep it from getting any worse."

"Brother and Sister Goodgion can vouch for me," Esther said. "That should put an end to it." Esther felt her face flush as hot anger boiled up in her.

"No, I think the least said the better. It will take a while to live this down and you must walk circumspectly. In the meantime, I'll talk to Ben and make sure his intentions are honorable."

"Pa, please don't do that!" She remembered Ben's quick temper that had resulted in the fight on the Fourth. "He asked me to walk out with him. I know he is an honorable man."

"What did you say?"

"I told him I couldn't answer him right now. He promised that he'd ask me again later."

"All right, then, I won't approach him. We'll do this for the time being; you won't go anywhere unless your mother or I accompany you. I know that seems drastic to you but I believe it to be best until this gossip dies down."

At church that morning Flora dropped into the seat Esther had saved for her. Esther's father had already moved to the front to lead singing so Esther only whispered, "I need to talk something over with you after church."

At the last 'amen', Flora pulled her aside and said, "Tell me. I'm dying to know."

Esther said, "First, Flossie, you have to promise you won't breathe this to a living soul. Cross your heart and hope to die."

Flora's face fell. "Can I tell Plez?"

"No, not a soul. Promise me."

Flora shook her head. "Essie, you're my best friend. Before I married, I'd have kept any secret you told me. But it's different now. I've never kept anything from my husband."

Esther had never felt so alone in her life. Even when Jed had married without warning, she had cried on Flora's shoulder. All Flora's sympathies in that instance had been with her friend rather than with her brother. But if Flora told Plez and he let something slip to Ben, Esther didn't know what Ben would do. Loath to take a chance, she told Flora, "Then I can't tell you. I'm sorry; I wanted to know what you think. But I'll have to figure it out by myself."

"Essie, you're killing me. You're making me more curious by the minute."

"Flossie, I'm sorry. Truly, I am. Maybe someday I'll tell you when I see how it all works out, but I can't take a chance now. Promise you'll still be my friend?"

Flora hugged her. "Of course, your friendship means too much to me. I'll tell you what, come go home with me for dinner. I fixed chicken and dumplings, your favorite. We'll have a good talk while Plez goes to his ballgame."

"It sounds good, but I guess I'd better not. Maybe another time."

After the noon meal, Esther and her mother cleaned up the kitchen while her father and the boys gathered around Beulah at the piano to practice. Keeping her voice low, Esther said, "Ma, did Pa talk to you about what he told me this morning?"

Judith nodded her head.

"Ma, I want to live this down as much as you and Pa do; no, more than you do. How strict do I need to be about going any place without you or Pa? Flora asked me to go home with her after church today and I thought I'd best ask you or Pa before saying yes. Do I have to give up my friends?" She started to cry, wiped the tears with a corner of her apron and snubbed.

"Oh, my dear," Judith said putting her arms around her. "We have to be so careful about what people will say. Don't you see if you go to Flora's that people will say you're meeting Ben there? I know, myself, that it would be all right for you to meet Ben there. But gossips with evil minds might make something of it. Invite Flora to come over here to see you."

The more Esther thought about it that week the less she thought that Flora would consent to coming over to spend the day. For one thing, she expected her baby just any day and Esther knew that she wanted to stay close to Plez. When the time came, she expected Lillie to stay with them for the two-week confinement to take care of both Flora and the baby. After that, her friend would be too busy to concern herself with Esther's troubles.

Too, her two older brothers seemed to look at her in a new light—not suspicion, exactly, more like a dawning realization that she had become a desirable woman. Esther felt tension between them and wished sometimes things could go back to the way they had been before they heard the gossip. Other times she enjoyed her new status and daydreamed of the time when, as a married woman, she would invite guests to visit her in her own home. She looked forward to having her own sphere in which she could make decisions and not be restrained by her strict, old-fashioned parents.

Over the past several months, she had squelched the memory of her confident expectations of marrying Jed until they seemed foreign to her nature. When his hurry-up wedding first occurred, she could think of nothing but his betrayal and had to be prompted to perform the most routine chores. She stopped appearing in public except for church services, sitting beside Flora as in the past but avoiding the other young people. As time went on, different members of the congregation experienced births, marriages, and sickness or death, and she accompanied her mother on calls of congratulation or condolence. Her old effervescent trusting spirit had vanished, but in its place she had developed a calm exterior and a genuine sympathy for others. She found that she had a knack for tending the sick and offered her services when needed.

A request for her to go help Mr. Pendleton's daughter pushed her into making a decision. The old gentleman had become even frailer since a bout of pneumonia the previous winter and required more care. When his daughter accidentally burned both hands so badly that she could do no work, they sent word to Esther asking that she stay with them until the wounds healed. Her parents refused to let her go.

Thinking the restriction far too rigid, Esther rebelled. Outwardly docile, she began plotting to escape. Dreams of running away and training to become a nurse gave way to more practical solutions and by Sunday she had made her plans.

Everett McMasters had announced the first song and Esther had begun to worry that her friend might not be able to help her fulfill her scheme when Flora lowered her swollen body to the seat next to her. Relieved, Esther let her voice soar. She scarcely heard the sermon and had a hard time concentrating on the prayers as she waited anxiously for the worship to end. As soon as the dismissal prayer ended, she pulled Flora aside.

"Flossie, will you do something for me?"

"If I can."

"Will you tell Ben I'd like to see him?"

Flora beamed. "*Will* I. Where do you want to meet him? At my house?"

"No, he'll need to come to our house. He can come any evening he gets a chance. I will be expecting him but I don't intend to tell my folks until I get to talk to Ben first. So tell him that my Pa may answer the door and not to let on that I sent for him."

On Tuesday evening after the sun went down, the day's work over, and supper finished, the McMasters family settled in the front yard to try to find a cool breeze. Late July days presented temperatures in the high nineties under a blazing sun and the thermometer receded little during the nights. That evening a light breeze from the east relieved the high humidity and discouraged mosquitoes. Arnold and Beulah spread a quilt on the dry grass and lay looking for stars to appear. The other members had carried chairs from the house.

Just before dark Ben Conover rode up on his horse. The men rose to meet him and showed him a porch post for hitching his mount.

"Arnold, go draw a fresh bucket of water so Ben can refresh himself after his ride. Beulah, go get another chair for Ben," Everett said. "Here, Ben, take my chair."

"Thank you, Mr. McMasters, I'll wait. I want to walk around a bit and stretch my legs. Sitting in the saddle even for this short distance stiffens me up."

McMasters laughed. "You're too young for that. Wait until you're my age."

Esther fidgeted in her chair. Social customs dictated that the young man visit with her parents and brothers when calling on her; her father acted as if Ben had come to see him. In no way would he let on that he recognized the real reason Ben had showed up on a workday evening; Ben would be required to make the first move.

Arnold arrived with a bucket of water and Ben took a long, appreciative drink from the dipper. Thanking Arnold, he turned to see Beulah carrying his chair and hurried to take it from her. Careful to place the chair far from Esther but in the circle so that he faced everyone, he addressed his remarks to Mrs. McMasters at first and then entered into general conversation with the men.

Near dark, he cleared his throat and spoke to Esther's father. "Mr. McMasters, with your permission and Esther's, of course, I'd like to ask Esther to walk down the lane with me."

Everett considered the request as if the fate of the world depended on his reply. "Ben," he said, "I believe I'll have to turn you down."

Esther's heart sank. Her carefully laid plans had come to naught.

But her father continued, "You have my permission to sit together in the porch swing."

When they sat in the porch swing within easy view of her parents, Esther tried to keep the anger from her voice as she said, "They're not letting me out of their sight."

"Why? Is it something to do with me?"

Esther hesitated. "You figure into it but not in the way you suppose. It's gossip. Have you heard nothing?"

"No, I haven't been anywhere to hear anything. I've been trying to clean up my pecan grove. It's been a mess. The ice storm in aught-four left limbs in the treetops broken and hanging down. Stump did nothing to clean them up. So all the little limbs that fell to the ground have undergrowth tangled through them. I have to climb the trees and saw off the broken branches. I'll try to straighten up the splits this winter after the sap goes down. So I've been getting up early, working all day, and falling into bed at night."

"You *have* been busy," Esther said. "It's just as well, though. I'd rather tell you myself. I heard it over two weeks ago and I've been trying to decide what to do. My folks might as well have put me in quarantine. They decided that I could not go anywhere without one of them along. Flora invited me home with her and I couldn't even go over there."

"Esther, get to the *point*. Tell me the gossip."

"I don't know for sure every bit of it; Pa didn't tell me. But that town boy you had the fight with at the picnic started it. Pa just said that he had made up all sorts of lies and spread the gossip around as fact. He said that our walking off from the picnic together seemed to be the basis for it."

Ben jumped up from his seat at the opposite end of the swing so suddenly that Esther had to hold on tight to keep from falling. He didn't seem to notice as he paced the length of the porch and back. "You've kept this from me for over two *weeks*," he said. "I'd have found this fellow and put a stop to it. I still can."

"That's partly the reason I didn't tell you. I figured you'd act this way. Pa thinks the best way to squelch these rumors is to live a circumspect life until it dies down. I think he may be right but I can't stand to live like this. I feel so tied down."

"I'm going to town tomorrow and hunt that chap down. He shouldn't be hard to find. I know him as a lazy, good-for-nothing street corner loafer. I'll shut his mouth."

"Ben, I beg you not to do that. It would just give him more fodder for his lies. He'd think there must be something to it or you wouldn't be so mad."

Ben stood in front of her, hand above his head clutching a porch post. "Do you have a better solution?"

He's so mad, Esther thought, I must calm him down. "Yes, I think I do, but you have to agree. Sit back down and let's talk about it."

Ben rejoined her, sitting a little closer. "Tell me."

"You asked me once to keep company with you. I think that is the solution, or to at least look to other people like we're keeping company."

"Are you saying you want me to call on you for real or pretend?"

"I don't know. I'd like to be able to go places and do the things the other young people do. I can't do that without an escort. I like you, Ben, and I like to be with you. You feel the same way about me, don't you?"

Ben didn't answer for a long time. He's probably trying to think of a tactful way to let me down easy, Esther thought. I probably said that all wrong. I have a hard time saying what I mean so that other people understand me.

Ben's voice sounded different when he spoke. "The same way? My feelings are deeper than just liking you. It sounds to me like you don't feel the same way about me. But I guess I understand and I'm willing to take my chances that closer acquaintance will make you fonder. Would you like me to speak to your Pa?"

Relief flowed through Esther like a quiet stream. "Oh, yes, Ben, would you?" She wanted to hug him. "I'll go tell him to come to the porch."

CHAPTER 10

Ben

Ben burst out in song on his way home. He sang the happy tune *Billy Boy* substituting his own name: Oh, where have you been, Benny Boy? Benny Boy? I have been to seek a wife. His horse didn't mind that he sang off key but, as Ben thought of Esther's beautiful voice, the song trailed off. Instead of singing, he whistled the tune. He had always been able to hear the melodies correctly in his brain but had trouble translating them to voice. Whistling, however, posed no such problem. He determined then and there to incorporate as many flourishes into his whistles as he could learn. Since childhood he had mimicked birdcalls. If he could master the song of the mockingbird he would present it to Esther as a gesture of his affection.

His pecan orchard presented the perfect place to study mockingbird song. A project of back breaking labor metamorphosed like a worm becoming a beautiful butterfly. He heard birds singing during the morning hours as he chopped at the stubborn tangle of briars amid saplings. When he saw a mockingbird light on the weathered pinnacle of a broken limb high in a tree he stopped and stood listening. Most times the bird rewarded him with its varied warble before flying straight up as if it could not contain its exuberance. If it returned to its lofty perch to sing more, he felt that he heard an encore.

In the heat of the day when no birds sang he worked with his father and Holt on the scraggly cotton crop. The spring floods had ravaged their land and they had little prospect of income for the year. His pecan trees had been neglected since the ice storm damage of 1904. They produced so little fruit that he expected to have no marketable crop. The small crop last year had barely supplied their needs. He sold the pecans that Holt and the girls picked so that they could have a little spending money but kept the rest. Next year would be different—every year held out hope for a good crop.

Each evening after supper, Ben returned to work clearing the undergrowth in his pecan grove. Daylight lingered until after nine o'clock that time of year. Through the hot, humid hours he grubbed out roots and stacked small limbs ready to burn as soon as rain made it safe. Sometimes a breeze came up after sundown to cool his sweaty back but always the homing birds filled him with peace as he dreamed of making a home for himself and Esther.

They established a routine of seeing each other on Sunday. He shied away from showing up at church—he felt it would be hypocritical—but called in the afternoon and they went to see Plez play baseball. Through August and into September Flora accompanied them but she soon became embarrassed by her obvious pregnancy and, telling them she felt it unseemly for her to appear in public except for church, left them to go alone. The season ended soon after that and Ben and Esther spent Sunday afternoons playing dominoes at Plez and Flora's house.

As weeks went by Esther regained her former sunny disposition. Although Ben ached to hold her in his arms, he restrained himself as he watched her become brighter each time they met. I had lots of practice bringing Ma out of her spells, he thought. I remember how good I felt when she began smiling more often. I'll just content myself being with a happy girl.

He marked time as summer passed and the anniversary of Jed's marriage approached. Having promised himself to wait a year to let Esther recover, he busied himself with hard work and counted the days.

CHAPTER 11

Jed

Jed worked every day—including Sunday—on his house. His mother agitated about doing any kind of work on the Lord's Day except that necessary for meals and the care of livestock. Even his Pa, who didn't hold strict religious objections, rested his animals that day and believed humans needed a respite as well. Jed felt a little bit bad about it himself but he didn't know which emotion dominated: guilt or rebellion. Nevertheless, he told himself and anybody else who would listen that he must finish the floor and be ready to move rock when the county fixed the road.

Ben helped him when he had time. The lumberman had extended Ben credit to buy the materials he had estimated he needed. Matt and Holt helped them to roof the cabin and frame the door and windows. Millwork doors and window sashes waited at the lumberyard until Jed got ready for them. Jed's arrangement to get McIntosh's barn loft floor relieved Ben of buying flooring.

Jed hated to use any more of Ben's good trees on this cabin. "After all," he told Ben, "it takes years to grow a tree big enough to make house logs. I have a hunch that you won't wait that long to need several of them."

He grinned as he said it even though his skin felt stretched tight across his jaws and he feared his bared teeth looked too much like a snarl.

Ben gave him a funny look and said, "I'm glad you brought it up. I've been tiptoeing around the subject." He stopped and cleared his throat.

Jed waited not knowing what to say.

Ben swallowed hard making a noise in his throat before he went on. "How do you feel about me courting Esther?"

Jed felt like he'd rather anybody else in the world courted Esther, but he knew that he had given up his rights when he married Vinnie.

He spaced his words out to make sure Ben understood him, hoping his inner turmoil didn't show on the surface. "The way I look at it, Ben, is that it's not up to me to say. I have a wife and child myself and I know that any right-thinking man wants a family someday. You go ahead with your life and leave me out of it."

Jed could tell his answer didn't completely satisfy Ben. But he continued looking straight into Ben's eyes until Ben dropped his gaze first.

"Okay, then," Ben said, "we'll leave it at that."

Jed had trouble sleeping that night. He ran his conversation with Ben— such as it was—over and over in his mind. I've got to get ahold of myself, he thought. Ben is my best friend and I knew in the back of my mind that he fell for Esther the first time he ever saw her. I guess I hoped down deep that she would remain true to me even after the way I betrayed her. How realistic is that? Grow up, Man.

The next morning he hunted Ben up before breakfast. Waiting until Holt and Ida went to the barn to milk, he said, "Ben, I think we need to talk."

Courteously, Ben stopped in his tracks and turned toward his brother. Apparently seeing the seriousness written on Jed's face, he said, "Let's go back in the dugout where it's cooler."

Jed still didn't know how to start and Ben said nothing. After a minute or two, Jed coughed, took a deep breath and said, "I didn't want to leave things between us the way we ended yesterday. I've been thinking; you're the best friend I have in the world and I want you to feel the same way about me."

Ben started to speak but Jed held up his hand. "Let me have my say first." He swallowed before he continued, "I want to give you my blessing to court Esther. I know you don't need it; that will be up to the two of you. But I want it to be out in the open between you and me." He hurried on before Ben could interrupt. "They had to drag me to the altar after I got Vinnie in trouble, but that boy of mine makes it all worthwhile. I wouldn't give him up for all the diamonds and rubies in this whole world. I think that after we get out on our own, Vinnie and I will make a go of it. I've watched Pa and Ma and I'll try to remember to imitate them. As time goes on, maybe it'll come naturally to me, too. So you go ahead with your life. Just stay my friend. Okay?"

Ben had tears in his eyes. When Jed held his right hand toward him, Ben ignored it as he wrapped his brother in a bear hug. Jed shed a few tears of his own as he felt the knot in his midsection melt. It's going to be all right, he thought; we won't ever have to mention this again.

In late August, Baxter Wilson sent Jed word to come to the store bright and early the next Monday morning. He thought Jed had a good chance of getting on the road crew that would be rebuilding the bridge over the creek and grading the road. The message came in midweek so Jed assessed the amount of work he wanted to complete on his house that week just in case he got the job.

He had been taking his time getting everything just so before he laid the floor. That way he could let trash and bark that fell from trimming the logs remain on the bare dirt because he planned to cover it all up. Inside chinking had been completed quite a while and he needed to point it up in places. He'd get Vinnie started on that while he worked on the floor.

The next morning Jed went to the woods and cut small logs and dragged them to his location. It took him until after dark to hue one side of them and put them in for sleepers. He didn't have enough nails to secure the flooring snug—only those used nails Ben had straightened while they were escaping all the turmoil during the flood. Considering the short time left for the work, he blessed the day that they had moved the flooring plank and stacked it beside his front door. He grinned and thought, I call it my front door when I have but one in the house. Someday, though, I intend to do more building on this cabin. Then we'll see if it's the only door.

He hadn't quite completed laying the subfloor by Monday morning but he knew if he got work that he could finish by lantern light. Pa had loaned him a wagon sheet to stretch over the opening where he intended to build his fireplace. As soon as he finished the floor, he could hang the door and install the two windows and they could move in. Vinnie had been faunching to move before that and now with the prospect of work and being gone all day, he thought it might be a good idea. Ma would loan them a bed, they'd use the rough worktable as an eating table, and would have to make do for all the other stuff they needed. But it's still hot summertime and Vinnie can cook in the yard, he thought. And, if I know her, she'll scrub that floor until it's white. That'll be easier to do with no furniture in it.

❧   ❧   ❧

Jed hired on with the road crew to work twelve hours at three dollars a day in good weather. He hoped to work on his cabin on bad days. It looked like a fortune to him. He calculated how much he could save at that kind of salary;

Vinnie started talking about what they could buy with it. I almost wish I hadn't told her how much I'm making, Jed thought.

At first he worked with pick and shovel digging footings for the new bridge. Drays hauling posts and timbers for supports, rock for riprap, and 3x12 planking kept a steady hum of activity up and down the road. As soon as the work progressed to actual construction of the bridge, Mr. Talent, the boss, had promised to give him a chance at working on the bridge itself. He had watched the men handling the road plows and saw the constant strain on both men and animals. I could do it, he thought, but I'd a whole lot rather my labor counts for something that will last a while. Roads wash out every time it rains but bridges built strong and stout outlast them by years.

At first, he didn't know any of the other workers. Before the week ended, he had become acquainted with Spud Carlson. "You don't need to know my real name; my Ma saddled me with it but I got me a nickname almost as soon as I heard it. I even go by Spud on my work papers." He jabbed Jed in the ribs and winked. "I bet Jed ain't you real name, either."

Jed grinned and said, "Yep, Jed's my real given name." From the look on Spud's face and his explosive laugh, he doubted Spud believed him.

Jed liked Spud more and more as he got to know him better. They had much in common: their ages matched and their sons had the same birth month. Spud understood Jed's urge to move into his own place because he himself had just moved out from his Pa's. He volunteered to go over on Sunday to help out. Also Spud had been working with Mr. Talent for several months as a bridge builder. He told Jed that he would show him the ropes.

The good weather held all that week. Mr. Talent told his men that most work crews worked every day including Sunday but that he believed he got more work done with men who had rested a day each week. He urged the men to "make a showing" so that the inspector would keep approving their day off.

Jed went to town Saturday night after work to buy the few supplies he needed to get his place ready for occupation. He thought how good it felt to have a few dollars just to buy nails and hinges. He borrowed his Pa's buggy so Vinnie could go with him to Wilson's General Store. She wanted everything she saw but he convinced her to just look and make a mental note of the things she just had to have. He even resisted buying a sack of candy "for the boy". Wait until he's old enough to eat it, he thought.

True to his word, Spud showed up at Jed's cabin on Sunday morning ready to work. Jed had risen at daybreak and finished nailing the sleepers in preparation for installing the flooring from McIntosh's barn. The two men stopped to eat when Vinnie brought food at noon. That afternoon Ben and Holt arrived to help in any way they could. Ben said he'd better confine his labor to fetching and carrying but Holt had his own hammer and settled beside Spud to lay flooring.

When, tired and hungry, they stopped at dark, the floor spread before their satisfied scrutiny from wall to wall, nailed in place and finished. Jed could hardly contain his gratitude.

"Spud, in just one week, you've become the best friend I've ever met," he said as he threw an arm about Spud's shoulders and gripped his hand. "Man, you know your way around a hammer and saw. Where did you ever learn all you know in your short life?"

Spud grinned as he said, "My Pa is a finish carpenter. I worked with him from the time I was a little shaver." He glanced around at the unfinished cabin. "Next Sunday we'll plan on hanging the doors and making the windows. Then you can move in."

Ben chimed in, "I'll go this week and pick up the door—there's just one. I made arrangements to put the door and window sashes on my bill. Figure out what lumber you'll need for jambs, sills, and window framing and I'll get that, too."

Jed said, "I'm starved. I know Ma and the girls have dinner waiting for us. We can make out a list while we're eating."

Spud declined. "I'd better get on home," he said. "I'll see you at work tomorrow. If you and your brothers can't figure out what you need, I'll help you with your list tomorrow."

The next morning, Mr. Talent called his men together before they started work. "Men," he said, "I've got an announcement to make. We're going to have two convicts working with us beginning today sometime. They have been in the county jail since their conviction on horse theft and the judge has decided to have them work out their sentence on the road. I don't know how they decided to give them to us but there isn't anything we can do about it. They will have a guard over them so we shouldn't have any trouble with them. I want all of you to mind your own business and we'll make it okay."

Jed's heart lurched as he felt a tremor of dread. "I hope it's not the Sexton brothers," he said in an undertone to Spud as they picked up their shovels. "I don't believe I can work with them under any circumstances, but I need this job in the worst way. What'll I do if it is them?"

Spud slid down the creek bank stopping his slide with his shovel. "I don't see the problem. Talent said they'd have a guard over them and for us to mind our own business."

"If it's the Sextons, they killed my brother. I haven't seen them since that time—a year come September. I have laid awake some nights dreaming of getting my hands on them. I don't know whether I can control myself or not."

Spud stopped stock-still with one foot on the shovel preparing to shove it down into the soft ground to dig a hole for one of the five posts to support the bridge framework. "Man, that is a problem," he said. "Maybe it won't be them."

"I hope you're right," Jed said, "but I've got a bad feeling about it. Oh, well, no sense in borrowing trouble." He began digging a hole for the middle post.

An hour later, he heard new voices as the guard arrived with his little detail. From his position in the creek bed, he couldn't see the men but he felt all his muscles tighten with apprehension.

Spud spoke from the hole next to him. "Just go on about your business and don't let them get to you."

"That's easier said then done," Jed said. "My mouth's so dry I need a drink of water."

"Just keep digging. They'll bring the water around pretty soon, anyway."

Jed kept his head down as he neared the bottom of the six-foot hole. Most of the soil in the hole had consisted of the red clay prevalent in the area. A small amount of sand from the creek bed sifted down from the top but didn't fill the hole. His shovel struck rock on the next thrust and he finished cleaning out the remaining clay and trimming the sides of the hole until they were vertical and neat before he climbed out.

He placed his fists in the small of his back and flexed his shoulders as he peered down into the hole Spud dug. "How are you coming along?" he asked. "I think mine is ready for the post."

"Nearly finished. Don't stick your head above the creek bed," Spud said. "Let's see if we can finish another hole apiece before we hear the noon whistle."

Jed found it almost impossible not to satisfy his curiosity, but he followed Spud's advice. In the short week he had known him, he had found the man to be solid and prudent. Time enough to face the men when they stopped for their noon break.

He attacked the next excavation with a vengeance and had neared exhaustion before he got enough control to settle into a steady rhythm. It felt good to break a sweat and have the sun beat down on his wet back. The day promised to be another hot one but he had worked out in the heat this whole summer. He knew, however, that by three o'clock he'd wish for shade.

Arnold McMasters, the water boy, came around with a bucket of water and dipper before long. Jed took a long drink and filled the dipper again. "What can you tell me about the convicts, Arnold?" he asked.

Excitement lit the boy's features. "It's the Sextons," he said. "I asked Mr. Talent and he told me to stay as far away as I could get from them. When I take them water, I give it to the guard and wait until he brings the bucket back to me. The other men are all talking about it, though. Will Baker lives not far from them and he told me something before Mr. Talent shut him up. It seems that Al got married while out of jail on bail. Looks like that woman must have been already pregnant because he has a new baby boy just about the age of your baby. He got in trouble carrying a handgun and they put him back in jail over at Ardmore until after his trial. He hasn't been home in six months and hasn't seen his wife and baby in all that time. In fact, he hasn't seen his baby at all."

"Better for the boy if he never sees his Pa," Jed said. "I hate to think that an innocent little baby has that to face in his life."

"Arnold, get on with your work and quit killing time." The voice shouting from the roadbed belonged to the straw boss.

Spud climbed out of the hole, and reached for the water dipper. He thanked Arnold for the drink and said, "Don't get yourself in trouble with the boss, Arnold. You're a good hand but it doesn't take much to ruin your chances of keeping your job these days."

When they stopped to eat their lunch, Jed noticed that the guard kept his prisoners separate. He appreciated that because he didn't want any truck with them.

But the distance didn't keep Al from running his mouth. He yelled to Will Baker, "Have you seen anything of my family?"

Mr. Talent held up a hand to stop any reply that Baker might have answered. "Don't say anything to him," he said. "That goes for all you men. We have to accept them on the crew when the court sends them out, but we don't have to have any conversation with them. I put them to pushing wheelbarrows of riprap and I'll keep the rest of you busy in the creekbed and shaking a road plow so you'll not be close to them."

Sexton didn't let Baker's lack of reply faze him. "Conover," he yelled, "what do you hear from your cowardly brother?"

Talent's stern look stopped Jed from saying anything back but he felt his hackles rise and bile fill his throat. When the whistle sounded calling them back to work, he went to Mr. Talent. "Mr. Talent," he said, "I don't know whether I can work around the men who killed my brother. I need this job something fierce and I sure do thank you for giving it to me, but I'm asking you if there is anything you can do to get rid of them."

When he saw Talent's look of compassion, Jed felt hot tears spring to his eyes. "No, Son," Talent said, "I have to take what they send me. But I'll keep you as far from them as I can and I'll let you work on the bridge so you'll be down in the creek and not have to see them very much."

Talent's compassionate words mollified Jed somewhat. He kept thinking about the brothers after he went back to work but didn't allow his thoughts to slow his work. Neither did he talk with his fellow workers. With several of them digging holes, they would be ready to set the ten round twelve-inch posts by midafternoon. Spud and Jed finished cleaning the holes they were digging before the last two workers completed the job.

Mr. Talent gave a cursory glance at the unfinished work and called to Spud, "You and Jed come on over here and I'll go over the bridge building process with you while we wait."

Jed followed him to the table displaying the plans and leaned over to study the blueprints, trying to keep his eyes focused and not look toward the convicts. He soon became so engrossed with the process as Mr. Talent explained construction of the clear span bridge that he forgot everything else. He saw that the round posts to be set today, after having the tops leveled, would be notched at the top to fit 3x12 girders extending the width of the bridge. A 3x12 plate on top of the posts formed the frame to support 6x12 stringers set two feet apart lengthwise. Across these joists 3x12 planks floored the bridge with another 3x12 the length of the bridge on each side to act as a barrier to keep wheeled traffic from falling off the edge. Both ends of the bridge would be walled with 3x12s and dirt filled in behind them to level the bridge with the road.

After explaining the construction, Mr. Talent left Spud and Jed studying the plans while he checked on the progress of the digging. Seeing it finished, Talent told his men. "Hold on until I can talk to the guard about moving the convicts away from the material storage area. Get a good drink while you wait. Carrying these poles is going to be hot and heavy work."

Jed stood a little apart from the men clustered around the water buckets and watched Talent approach the guard who sat on a fallen log with his shotgun across his knees. He saw the guard turn toward Talent moving his eyes away from his surveillance area. In that split second, Al Sexton headed at top speed for the woods on the south side of the road dodging back and forth as he ran.

Jed yelled a warning, but instead of noticing the fleeing felon both Talent and the guard looked at Jed. Jed waved his arms and pointed at Sexton.

The guard whirled and raised his shotgun letting fly with both barrels just as Sexton reached the woods. The guard dropped the weapon and quickly unholstered his sidearm but saw immediately that he had no use for it. Al Sexton had fallen on his face into a tree and lay still.

Camp Sexton had turned to watch his brother run but had made no move to follow. When he saw Al fall he started toward him but after one step he stopped and raised his arms above his head.

The guard approached Camp with handcuffs at the ready. Jed could not hear the order but he saw Camp nod and walk ahead of the guard past his brother's body. The guard holstered his pistol and reloaded the shotgun. With the shotgun trained on Camp, he knelt and made certain that Al Sexton had indeed died. Then he marched Camp to the wagon used to transport prisoners and handcuffed him to the bars.

Approaching Talent, he said, "If I can have the use a couple of your men to load the body, I'm going back to Ardmore. I expect you have seen the last of us."

Spud and Baker lifted Al Sexton onto the wagon and one of the other men brought the horses and settled them in the shafts. Mounting the wagon seat, the guard departed.

"All right, Men," Talent said. "Let's get back to work. We've got lots of daylight left and we need to pack those posts in before we quit today. It looks like rain and I'd a whole lot rather have it help settle that red clay than to have ten holes full of water."

CHAPTER 12

Ben

As winter came on and the farm work slowed down, many of the neighbors hosted parties of one kind or another. One Sunday evening in late fall Polly Wilson invited a group of youngsters to her home to gather around the piano and sing. They sang religious songs and old favorites while Polly accompanied them on the piano. If she didn't know the song they sang a cappella. Not trusting his singing voice, Ben whistled softly. Esther's lips parted in her sunny smile and he could tell she liked to hear him whistle.

Some new church members had recently moved into the community from St. Louis and the friendly son and daughter soon became an integral part of the young people's fellowship. Rather than looking down on the country people because they had come from a big city, they taught them dancing games to the peppy tunes of new songs. The Wilsons' large home afforded room for long lines required by some of the games. Because the party occurred on Sunday, even those who held no religious scruples agreed to skip instead of dance so that everyone could participate.

Ben watched the new man and, considering that he seemed to be trying to ingratiate himself with the ladies and girls, began to speculate about his age. He had a boyish face but acted older, regarding Esther with what Ben considered boldness. Surely he can tell she's with me, Ben thought.

As he watched the young man sidle closer to Esther, Ben decided to put the quietus on his actions. He stepped between the man and Esther and extended his hand in greeting. "I don't believe we've been made acquainted," he said. "My name's Ben Conover."

Smiling broadly, the man took his hand. "Phillip Atchison," he said. "I haven't seen you at church, have I?"

It's not that big a congregation, Ben thought; he knows I haven't been there. Matching Phillip's smile, he said, "I'm sure you have met my mother and sisters, Mrs. Conover and Mrs. Wilson and Ida and Betsy."

Phillip dropped his gaze to their hands and disengaged his own. Score one for me, Ben thought, I stared him down.

"Oh, yes, fine family," Phillip said.

Ida edged in between Ben and Phillip. With her back to Phillip, she winked at Ben and then turned toward Phillip. "I came over here to introduce you two but I see you have taken care of that yourselves. Mr. Atchison, I have been accused of being brazen before, so it won't surprise anybody if I ask you to be my partner for this reel they've just announced."

Atchison chuckled and took her hand. "Miss Ida, I'd be honored," he said as he led her to the end of the line that had formed in the dining room.

At the end of the party Polly announced a candy breaking. She brought out a large deep box with a hole in the top barely big enough for a hand to pass through it. The boys chose partners and then each partner reached into the box and brought forth a stick of candy. If the sticks matched in color and flavor, they kept both sticks. If not, they put one stick back and shared the other stick by breaking it. They repeated the process until no more candy remained.

When Ben and Esther captured matching pieces the first time they grappled, everyone clapped because they were the first couple to do so. But when they brought out matching sticks the third time, some of the boys started teasing Ben. "You are so well matched that you can't even draw candy that doesn't match. You'd better ask her to marry you, Ben." Esther's face and neck turned a deep crimson but she giggled. Ben thought she liked the joshing and he certainly didn't mind. They drew twice more and each time got matching candy. I wonder how that makes Mr. Atchison feel, Ben thought. I hope that between us, Ida and I have nipped his intentions in the bud.

Ben made arrangements to pick up his horse on the way back from walking Esther home. Beulah had stayed home that evening because of a bad cold so he and Esther were alone. That late November night a full moon graced the sky and moonlight filtered through the oak leaves that still clung to the trees alongside the road. The temperatures of a warm day had declined as night fell; Esther shivered in her lightweight wrap. Ben took off his coat and spread it across her shoulders. Letting his hands linger as he straightened it, he said, "I have a little present for you."

"Oh, Ben, you shouldn't have," she said. "I know you're having a hard time now with it being such a bad crop year."

"It cost me no money," he said. "I want you to see if you can guess. I'll give you a clue and you guess. Then I'll give you another clue, and so on and so on." He had stopped in the middle of the road but about ten yards ahead he spied a stump just the right height to make a good seat. "Come sit on that stump yonder. This may take a while."

She sat willingly on the stump while he stood before her. He could tell she liked the little game he had concocted when she said, "What's the first clue?"

"I already gave it to you," he said.

"Oh, that it cost no money. Is it something you made?"

"I ask the questions; you give the answers," he said. "That's the way it works."

She squirmed a little on the stump and pushed a pointed forefinger against her head as if in deep thought. "It's a sewing box."

"Jed is the woodworker, not me. Second clue: I give it to you but I keep it for myself."

In the bright moonlight, he could see that her face glowed. She's blushing, he thought. She hesitated and he urged, "Go ahead, say it. I won't tell anybody." I'm enjoying this no end, he thought.

"Okay, is it a hug?"

"Nope, but that sure is a good idea. We could save my surprise for another time if you want to try a hug now."

"Ben, quit bedeviling me. Give me another clue."

"It won't embarrass you. At least I don't think it will. It's musical in a way."

"Ben, tell me; I can't stand this. I'll never guess."

She sounded like an anxious little child. Ben took both of her hands and lifted her up from her seat. Still holding both hands, he began softly to trill the long warble of the mockingbird song switching to a louder whistle as he repeated two sharp notes and then dropping to a harsh chirr before building to a crescendo as he ended the varied medley.

Esther dropped his hands and hugged him. "Oh, Ben, that is so beautiful. You couldn't have given me anything that pleased me more."

Ben took advantage of her hug to encircle her with his arms and hold her tight. She didn't resist; instead she leaned back to look him in the eye. "You know what we could do? We could work up a duet with me singing *Listen to the Mockingbird* and you whistling the bird's song. What do you think?"

I think you're the most beautiful sight that I've ever beheld in the moonlight, he thought. "I'm all for it," he said. "It would take a lot of practice, wouldn't it?"

She giggled. Ben stroked the hair that fell down her back. She had never let their relationship progress this far before. Tangling her hair in his hands, he pulled her head back and bent to kiss her.

She twisted out of his arms as if propelled by a demon. "Don't," she said in a strangled voice.

"I'm sorry. I thought you wanted the kiss as much as I did."

"It's just…. It's something I can't explain. I didn't mean to be so forward when I hugged you but I was so carried away with your present. Can't we just go on the way we were?"

"No, I don't think we can. I can't keep on seeing you and not touching you. I won't do anything to disrespect you—you know that. But I want to hold you and caress you. I want to make you love me the way I love you."

She remained silent. He cast about in his mind for a reason for her reaction. I'll just question her until I find out, he thought. "Is the reason you won't kiss me that we're not betrothed?"

She nodded.

He thought a long while about how to explain his position. "Esther," he said, "I'm not in a position to ask you to marry me right now. I'm deep in debt; I borrowed money from the bank to buy my land and I owe a bill at the lumberyard for Jed's house. The note at the bank is due and I don't have a penny to pay on it. I hope that the bank will understand about this year's bad crop but I don't know. So you can see what a bind I'm in."

"Ben," she said, "I don't mind a long engagement. You have no idea how much work it takes to get ready for a wedding. I'd have to make my wedding dress and piece some quilts and gather some more things for my hope chest…."

He couldn't believe his ears. "Are you saying that you will marry me?"

"Yes, if you want me."

As he took her in his arms he smelled the faint violet fragrance of her dusting powder. In after years, the scent always brought the brightness of full moon and the crisp feel of cold November nights to mind. She lifted her face for his kiss.

"I love you so much," he said. "Tell me you love me."

"I admire you and respect you, Ben. I'll make you a good wife. We'll have a good life together."

Ben had never felt such disappointment in his life. His gut twisted and heaviness filled his chest. He let his hand slide down her arm and clasped her hand. "I'd better get you on home," he said.

Holding hands, they walked side by side down the lane. As they neared her house, she said, "Ben, does this mean you don't want to marry me?"

He stopped in his tracks and wrapped her in his arms again. "Essie, I still want that more than anything in the world. I wish you could tell me you love me but I know how honest you are and I admire you for it. I love you enough for both of us. It'll be all right. I just wish we could marry now instead of having to wait until I can afford it. That may take years."

NOVEMBER, 1918

CHAPTER 13

Esther

Esther held the kerosene lamp above her head to spread the light in a wider circle and looked down at her sister-in-law as she lay sleeping. Vinnie had drifted into an uneasy slumber about an hour earlier and Jed, exhausted from a week of caring for her while he recuperated from the same illness, had retreated to the front room leaving Esther to sit by the bedside. Vinnie's restlessness had subsided soon after Jed left the room and her sleep became peaceful. When her breathing settled to an even rhythm, Esther felt her forehead and found it cool to the touch.

As she reflected on the three weeks just past, Esther breathed a silent prayer to be spared this terrible sickness that had invaded the nation and entered most of the homes of the people she knew and loved. She and Ben had not fallen ill but their own little Matthew had not fared as well and only the past day or two had felt well enough that she dared be away from him even for a few hours.

She set the lamp on the dresser in front of the mirror to enhance the amount of light and fitted a postcard around the base of the globe between two prongs to keep the light out of Vinnie's eyes. Satisfied that she could safely leave her sister-in-law alone in the room, she moved into the front room herself. Finding the fire burned down to coals, she added two logs and poked it into a blaze. The hands on the carved kitchen clock on the stone mantle of the fireplace pointed to 4:30. About the time she and Ben had married nearly eight years ago, Jed had carved the clock using one he borrowed from Plez and Flora as a guide. Inserting cheap works he had purchased at Wilson's store, he had disguised them in such a way that they completed a beautiful clock.

Noticing the clock caused her to look around at all the things Jed's hands had fashioned. She had not seen the fireplace before tonight although she had been told many times what a good job Jed had done in building it. Built of limestone, it covered half of the wall in both width and height. One large stone artistically chipped in an even pattern around the edges served as a mantle. Jed had engineered the fireplace so that the firebox and the chimney worked so well together that a small fire warmed the room except in the coldest weather.

As Esther studied the care and attention with which Jed had laid each stone, the icy core of her heart thawed a little. In all the years since she had read his note on the day of Flora's quilting bee, she had harbored resentment toward Vinnie. She had to admit that Jed received his share of her bitterness.

With difficulty she pushed the memory down to its customary place deep in the recesses of her mind. I'll think of something else, she thought.

Staring into the fire as it began to catch and leap up, she formed pictures from stories she had been told about the way Jed built the house without having any money to pay for it.

Back in aught-eight after the flood, he had swapped work for much of the stone that went into this very fireplace. She knew that Ben and the rest of the men had worked on tearing down the old barn he used for flooring and hauling those planks and this stone to his location. But Ben had told her that Jed worked from daylight until way after dark every day.

After he got the job with the county road crew, he built the house on Sunday and evenings after he got home from work. She thought about his working twelve hours a day on the roads, then coming home and working by lanternlight until he fell in bed exhausted. He had used a small amount of his wages to buy nails to secure the flooring better and to purchase hinges for the door but had managed, as he said, for the balance of his house. His family needed so many things.

That year, Ben had started during the summer to clean out his pecan orchard. The job lasted until hard winter and he still found no stopping place. Matt and Jed had hauled the small logs Ben had cut off the trees to Jed's place and used them to build a fire to burn limestone to point up the chimney. Mr. Pendleton had been a stonemason in the old days and supervised the job although he did no work on it because of his age. Jed told Ben that he learned so much from the old man that he would be eternally grateful for his help.

The county allowed Jed to use their equipment to clear an access lane from the cabin to the county road and furnished and set a tinhorn across the ditch. By moving the solid large stone along the section lines and down this lane, he managed to keep it in one piece to use for the mantle. Before setting it, he chipped a design along the edges. As Ben told her, he put lace on it the way he did everything he built.

She knew that he and Vinnie had lived a hardscrabble existence. The woman could throw more out the back door than Jed brought in at the front door, she thought, and felt pity for the man who had broken her heart so long ago. He had made the best of the poor situation created when he and Vinnie had to get married.

Ben thought that Jed had never got along with Vinnie the way husbands and wives should do. Jed spent almost every evening in the workshop he and Holt had set up in their father's barn. Ben said Jed used teaching Holt as an excuse when Vinnie complained.

Looking around the room, Esther saw furniture he had made with his own hands and thought the quality surpassed much of that found in manufactured pieces. She had to fight against coveting the oak dining room set. It had eight chairs to go with the harvest table and sideboard. It took up much of the space in the kitchen area but they used the chairs in other parts of the small room. Other than those chairs, they had two overstuffed living room chairs.

She and Ben had already been married when Jed made a deal for the oak lumber he used for the set. Ben had given him two large walnut trees which they cut down and loaded one at a time on a wagon. Jed had spent a week each time hauling the logs to a distant sawmill using his Pa's mules to pull the wagon. There he traded the walnut logs for enough seasoned oak planks to fashion the whole set. Word had it that a sawmill operator had to set a watch on the valuable walnut logs or someone would steal them. Esther found that hard to believe; farmers knew how walnut trees didn't allow anything to grow under them.

Esther turned around with her back to the fire and saw that Jed had fallen asleep in his chair. A black curl from the tangled mass of his thick hair tumbled over his forehead. His long black lashes brushed his pale cheeks and emphasized the dark circles under his eyes. She tried without success to suppress the thrill that gripped her. Tiptoeing into the bedroom, she found a quilt to cover him. After warming it in front of the fire, she spread it over him, gently tucked it around him and stood looking down at him. They hadn't been alone in the eleven years since Jed married. Poor boy, she thought with compassion long buried, he looks so worn out.

Jed jerked awake and started up out of his chair colliding with Esther as she tried to back away. They both stumbled and righted themselves by grabbing at each other. She saw his chin quiver and tears slide down his cheeks. He put his arms around her and buried his head against her neck. She held him the way she comforted her own little Matthew when his childish heart felt some real or imagined pain.

"Oh, Essie, Essie," he said.

She heard the pain and weariness in his voice, felt his tears against her skin, and stroked his neck until she felt the tension drain from him. When she moved to step away, his arms tightened around her and he kissed her neck.

Esther said, "No, Jed, no." She put her hands against his chest and tried to push him away.

He took her face in one hand and looked into her eyes. "Don't look at me like that if you want me to let you go, Essie," he told her. "I can tell you want me as much as I want you."

She closed her eyes and willed her heart to still its wild beating. It filled up her chest until she had no room for air. She caught her breath as she felt Jed's lips close on hers. For an instant her body sagged against him and she felt his arms squeeze her. Conscious-stricken, she wrenched her mouth from his and pushed him away again.

"No, Jed, please let me go."

He dropped his arms then and turned and walked to the window. Breaking daylight outlined his form as he stood droop-shouldered and defeated. How tired he is, Esther thought. I just want to put my arms around him again and comfort him. Then in disgust she thought, Comfort him? Ha! I just want my arms around him and feel him holding me close again.

Jed's slumped shoulders straightened as if a ramrod had been thrust down his spine. He turned away from the window and strode back to her.

"Essie," he said, "I haven't said one word to you in all these years since Vinnie and I married. I never even knew if you got my note I left you that day. I thought you hated me. But I know better now. A woman just doesn't look at a man the way you're looking at me now unless she feels something for him. Esther, you can't tell me you don't love me."

"Hush, Jed. What if Vinnie or your children wake up and hear us?" Esther looked guiltily from the cot in the corner of the room where J. C. slept deeply to Vinnie's bedroom.

Moving closer to her, Jed shook his head and grinned. "That's my Essie, always caring what other people think," he said in a stage whisper.

It made her mad. "You're asking me to throw away everything I have believed in all my life, let alone betray my husband, your brother."

"Esther, I'm just trying to get you to be honest. Can't you face a few facts? You know I have never loved Vinnie. And I know now you don't love Ben. Not in the way he deserves. You didn't love him when you married him. You care more about what people think than you do about yourself or me."

Tears filled her eyes and she held up her hand to stop him.

But he couldn't be stopped. "I've done the best I can; I've tried to make it up to Vinnie that I couldn't love her. She's a better person than any of you think. I feel like the devil himself thinking of you when I'm with her. But I can't help loving you. I always have since the first time I ever saw you. You know it's true. I told you in my note that I'd always love you. Did you get my note?"

Esther thought of the note hidden all these years in the picture frame behind the family picture taken shortly after Beulah's birth. Although she knew every word by heart, she took it out and read it from time to time when she knew no one would catch her. Her heart turned over now as she remembered the two words: 'Know this'.

She stood mute as she nodded her head.

"I love you," Jed's voice deepened. "Vinnie and Ben both know that deep down. I know you love me, too. Are we going to have to pay for the rest of our lives for one mistake I made? I don't fault you—I'm the only one to blame—but Essie, don't you think we have both paid enough? It's been eleven years; that's long enough."

He took her by the shoulders and forced her to lift her eyes until she looked into his. "Just say it one time," he said. "Just say you love me."

Esther saw the love and pain in Jed's eyes and knew her eyes reflected the same feelings. After all these years I thought I had it all under control, she thought. It doesn't matter. None of it matters. I still love him.

She twisted out of his grasp and faced away from him. Her voice sounded strangled, "Jed, you and I are brother and sister-in-law and will be for the rest of our lives." I can't face him, she thought, but I must. He'll never believe me if I don't.

She turned back and looked him full in the face. Daybreak through the window behind her lit his face. She saw the stubborn set of his jaw and knew she would never convince him. "Maybe I can't help the way I feel about you," she said. "And right now I can't control the way I look at you. But, Jed, I can help what I do about it. I married Ben with both eyes wide open, a grown woman knowing the consequences of her actions."

Jed opened his mouth as if to speak, but she shook her head. She extended her hand toward him but drew it back. I can't touch him, she thought.

"Jed, think about this a minute. We aren't the only ones involved. We have to think about the innocent children we have brought into the world. And Ben. You know there is nobody like Ben. He loves me and I am not going to do anything that will hurt him. Vinnie…" She glanced toward the bedroom where Vinnie lay in a deep sleep. "Well, I can't help feeling bitter toward Vinnie, but maybe someday I'll even get over that."

I'm doing the right thing, she thought, the one right thing. Her confidence made her voice stronger. "Maybe I don't face facts. I don't think any woman does, altogether. But women are practical, Jed. What good would it do to put it into words? What could come of it? I'm not going to leave Ben. You have Vinnie and three children to think about. Some things are better left unsaid. It's better just to leave things the way they have been, Jed. Much better."

Jed refused to accept defeat. "You're right about anything coming of it, but I know now you still love me. I just want to hear you say the words one more time. I'll beg if I have to. Please, Essie, just say you love me."

A lump rose in her throat and tears spilled down her cheeks. She looked at him silently through the tears.

Jed said, "I'll stand here and wait. You'll have to come to me."

She shook her head and ran to the outside door. Her coat hung on a peg beside it. Grabbing it and shrugging it on as she ran, she left the house without looking back. Once out of sight of the house, she slowed to a walk and trudged the half-mile home. Regret for refusing to say the words Jed wanted to hear and confidence that she had done the right thing fought to a draw. It's heart against head, she thought. I've always had that struggle, but head has always won. But, oh, how much I wanted to tell him that I still love him. I thought I had gotten over it but I have to admit I haven't. At least I didn't make the sin worse by saying the words.

CHAPTER 14

Esther

As she approached her home, she saw that smoke rose from both kitchen and fireplace chimneys. She had not expected Ben to start the fire in the wood cook stove; that chore had always fallen to her. But, she thought, this is the first time I have spent the whole night away. Still she wondered why he didn't use the new gas range if he needed to cook something. However, she thought, I like to cook on the old familiar wood myself.

She didn't give it much thought, though, because of the events of the previous night. During the illness that had felled first Jed, then Vinnie, she had managed to help in other ways rather than go to their house. Little Matthew had been sick with the same illness and had required her nursing during the two weeks Jed had been so ill before Vinnie came down with it. But last night everyone else in their two families had been unable for one reason or another to sit the night with Vinnie. Matthew's fever had been down for a week and she had run out of excuses so had taken her turn.

Fatigue overwhelmed her when she reached her own back door. She slumped against it and let the emotions and nursing duties of the night just past drain from her. I'll go in and flop on the bed in a minute as soon as I get the strength, she thought. If I can just sleep till noon, I think I'll make it.

Suddenly the door opened inward and she fell headlong onto the kitchen floor. Ben stooped over her. "Are you hurt?" he asked as he lifted her to her feet. "I'm sorry. I didn't know you were there. I didn't hear you come up." He led her to a chair. "I needed to go to the well to draw a bucket of fresh water.

Matthew has been vomiting off and on during the night. He finally fell asleep and I thought I'd grab a chance to bring in more water."

All thought of sleep fled as she hurried to her son's bedside. She removed the cloth Ben had placed on his forehead and laid her cheek against Matthew's cheek. Surprised at the coolness when she had expected fever, she went to the window and raised the shade in order to have a better look at him.

The five-year-old stirred and whimpered, "Mama."

"Mama's right here, baby," she said and smoothed his head and face with her hand. She felt his body convulse and grabbed the chamber pot as he retched. He lay back against the pillow exhausted and fell asleep.

Ben returned with the fresh, cool water, filled the wash pan, and brought it to her. She wet the cloth in it and, after washing the child's face, rinsed and wrung out the cloth before she laid it back on Matthew's forehead.

"When did he get so sick?"

Ben said, "About midnight. I let him sleep with me last night. He rolled over against me and woke me up. He got up and started stumbling around and talking out of his head. Then he started vomiting. I didn't know what to do. I couldn't leave him to go get you. I gave him half an aspirin but he couldn't keep it down. I didn't know what else to do. I kept him cleaned up as best I could and washed his face with cool water. When he went to sleep, I wrung out a rag and put it on his forehead the way I'd seen you do."

He knelt beside her chair, put his arms around her, and laid his head on her shoulder. "I'm so glad you're home, Honey. I don't know what I'd do without you."

Esther felt as if her legs and arms were made of lead. Her backbone seemed to have turned to rubber and her brain filled with fog. She laid her cheek against the top of Ben's head and let her exhaustion seep into his body. Strange how familiar this feels, she thought. For some reason, Ben had calmed her and eased her tension all their married life by holding her body close to his. Often starting as a different kind of closeness than passion, sometimes it changed to that. Ben always knows what I need, she thought.

He said, "You get undressed and ready for bed. You haven't had any sleep. Lie down here beside Matthew while I go do the morning chores. If you go to sleep, I know you will wake up if he needs you."

She hadn't realized that she still had her coat on until Ben lifted her to her feet and started unbuttoning it. I am tired, she thought, I didn't even take my coat off. She said, "I'll take my shoes off but keep my dress on. I don't think I'll go to sleep. You go and milk and feed. Have you had any breakfast?"

"I drank some milk and ate some leftover cornbread. I'm all right." He grinned. "Soon as I get some coffee I'll perk right up."

His attempt at humor elicited a small smile from Esther. "Go on," she said. "I'll have some coffee made when you get back."

She had breakfast on the way and poured a cup of hot coffee as soon as she heard Ben stomping his feet on the old rag rug inside the back door. "It's looks like the weather's going to get bad," he said. "Dark clouds coming in from the northwest and a norther just hit. After breakfast I'm going back out and pen all the animals up so they'll be easy to take care of the next few days. There's no telling how long it will last this time of year. When I get back, I want you to go to bed and get some rest. I'll look after Matthew."

Esther checked the oven and found the biscuits beginning to brown. She lifted fatback from boiling water where she had parboiled it, dredged it in flour, and dropped it into a skillet of hot grease where it sizzled and sent up an aroma that caused Ben to inhale a sound of pure pleasure. He's doing his best to cheer me up, Esther thought. She set the table and placed butter, sand plum jelly, and cream in the center. "How do you want your eggs this morning?"

When he said, "Over easy," she forked the fatback onto a platter and poured most of the grease into a can of drippings on the cabinet. Careful to keep any grease from igniting, she set the large skillet back on the burner, broke five eggs into it, salted and peppered them, and turned them over when the edges formed a brown lace. She set the platter of meat and eggs in front of Ben and pulled the biscuit pan from the oven.

"You're not eating any eggs this morning?" Ben teased.

"I'm going to try to eat one," she said. "I fixed enough meat and biscuits for you to have a cold dinner if I don't wake up in time. I thought a big breakfast might tide you over."

Ben looked disappointed that his attempt at humor had failed to spark a response. I'll blame it on tiredness, she thought. I can't let him find out about the temptation I've been through this night.

A knock at the kitchen door saved her from explanation. Ben scooted his chair away from the table to answer it, but the door opened letting in a blast of cold air as Matt entered and pushed the door shut behind him.

"Pa, what are you doing out in this kind of weather?" Ben asked. "Come on in by the fire and get warm."

Matt hovered near the kitchen range holding his hands over it and rubbing them together. Esther hurried to get another cup from the cupboard and poured him a steaming cup of coffee. Matt warmed his hands around the cup before he sat down and added a generous splash of cream.

"Sit down and have some breakfast with us," she said.

"Thank you, I had breakfast before I started out. I'll just stand here by the stove until I get warm. Lillie sent me to check on all her children. You'd think you were all still babies. She's particularly worried about Jed and Vinnie. You sat up last night, didn't you, Esther? How did you leave them?"

"Vinnie's fever broke during the night. She thrashed around some at first, but about four this morning she started sleeping naturally. I think she'll start to improve now. Jed is still weak and tired from looking after Vinnie since he got better, but I don't think you need to worry about him." She busied herself cutting up her meat and buttering another biscuit. Don't let them see any change in me, she prayed.

Matt poured coffee into his cup to heat it and sat at the table with them. "The weather hadn't changed much when I started out, but it is worsening fast. I don't think I'll go on down to Jed's. Rain is beginning to fall and freezing as fast as it hits. I've warmed up now and as soon as I finish this coffee, I'll head on back home. I wouldn't want my horse to slip."

After Matt left, Ben went to the barn to fasten his animals inside and provide them with hay for the pending cold snap. He would break ice on the pond and lead them to water once a day until the treacherous footing thawed.

Esther stole into the bedroom to check on Matthew. He hadn't vomited since before she started to cook breakfast. He slept now and didn't move when she laid her hand on his forehead to check his temperature. His skin still felt cool to her touch and although something struck her as odd about the way he lay in the bed, she couldn't put her finger on it.

She went back to the kitchen and washed the breakfast dishes, strained that morning's milk into the churn, and set it behind the stove to sour. This time of year the cows gave less milk and she didn't need to churn this day.

By the time Ben returned from his morning chores, her head felt like it had turned to wood. She said, "I put biscuits and fatback in the warming oven. Can you make out on that while I try to get some sleep? I'll crawl in beside Matthew so I can feel him if he stirs."

Ben came and put his arms around her. She flinched and drew back before she caught herself. Memory of Jed's embrace flooded her being but long habit of squelching all thought of him stood her in good stead. She leaned into her husband and put her aching head against the side of his neck.

He smoothed her hair and murmured, "Don't worry about me. You go get some rest."

"Go to the cellar and get a jar of peaches. That will help you piece out your dinner. When I wake up, I'll see if Matthew will eat some, too. He loves them so. I'll wait till you get back to be sure you don't slip and fall."

Ben kissed her cheek. "My little worrier," he said. "I'll be right back."

Esther's head had scarcely hit the pillow before she slept. She awoke to the sound of sleet against the window and awareness of chill in the room. Leaning on one elbow, she looked at her son. She thought he had not changed position since she checked on him right after breakfast.

"Ben," she called.

He jerked the door open and asked, "What's the matter? You sound scared."

"What time is it? I don't think Matthew has moved since I lay down. That scares me."

"I heard the clock strike three just a few minutes ago. You've been asleep five or six hours."

"I'm going to wake him up and see if he'll eat something." She laid her hand on the child's shoulder and shook him gently. "Wake up, Young Matt. Mama's gonna fix you something to eat."

He didn't stir. She shook him again, a little harder. Then, putting both hands beside him on the bed, she bounced it a few times. He opened his eyes, sat up and stared at a spot across the room. He tried to talk but words didn't form.

Ben ran to the kitchen and came back with a cup of water. He sat on the bed on the other side of Matthew, cradled the child in his left arm, and held the cup to his lips.

Matthew gulped the water and Ben pulled it away from his lips. "Easy, Cowboy," he said. "Swallow that and I'll give you another sip." Matthew drank the cup of water and licked his lips.

He hadn't changed his stare from the spot across the room. "J. C.," he said. "I'm ready to go. Have you got your gun?"

Esther's heart fluttered in her chest. She looked from Matthew to Ben. Ben looked as uneasy as she felt. But he hugged the child to him and said, "J. C. isn't here, Cowboy. He's at home with his Mama and Daddy."

"No, no, he's here, Daddy. He's right over there. Can't you see him?"

Esther sat back down beside the child and took his hands in her own. "Look at me, Matthew." The tone of her voice when she gave the order seemed to penetrate. He moved his head in her direction but kept his eyes turned toward the spot where he thought his cousin stood. "Matthew," Esther's tone sharpened. "Look me in the eye."

When she had his attention, she said, "Sweetie, you've been dreaming. You had such vivid dreams that you didn't know when you woke up. You're here in your bed and Mama and Daddy are right beside you. There's nobody else here."

Matthew screamed at her, "No, no, no. J. C. is right over there. I can see him plain as day. But he won't talk to me. He just stands there grinning and won't say a word. I think he's afraid of y'all. Wait, I'll ask him." He turned and looked at the figure he saw in his hallucination. "Is that why you won't answer me, J. C.? Do you want them to leave the room?"

Apparently he thought he had received an answer. "Go on, get out of here," he turned from one of his parents to the other.

Esther felt helpless. Ever since her teenage years she had nursed sick people. She felt she had a knack for it and never refused to help anyone who called on her unless her family needed her more at home. But she had never encountered anything resembling her son's illusion. She looked at her husband for guidance.

"Go fix him something to eat," he said. "I've had a lot of experience with people talking out of their head. Remember Ma had spells for a long time. Then after Paul's death Pa went through that black period. I'll see what I can do with Matthew."

When she returned with a small dish of cut-up peaches, Matthew lay back on his pillow with his eyes closed. Ben raised him to a sitting position and turned him in the bed so that the child leaned against him. Patting the child's face, he said, "Look here, Partner, your Mama brought you something good to eat."

Matthew opened his eyes and looked toward her with a dull stare. He's gone blind, she thought, and sucked in her breath with a sharp sound. Ben fixed her with a cautioning look and shook his head but Matthew appeared not to have heard.

She sat beside him on the bed and raised a spoonful of fruit to his lips. "Just taste this," she said. "It's your favorite, good canned peaches."

Matthew kept his lips closed tight.

Esther dropped the peaches back in the dish and, dipping a little juice with the spoon, she dribbled a few drops on his lips, thinking he would lick it off. But he ignored the sticky sweet while it dripped onto his chin. Esther squeezed water from the washcloth with one hand and wiped his face. Tears choked her as she said, "He isn't going to eat anything. Ben, I don't know what to do."

His father eased Matthew back down on his pillow where the child lay unmoving. "I don't know, either, Essie. I guess we just watch him. If he's not better by the time this weather thaws, I'll go get the doctor. I don't think I can make it to town with everything so iced up."

CHAPTER 15

Ben

Three days later when the ice melted, Matthew had improved to the point that they decided not to go for the doctor. The raging influenza epidemic had forced all the doctors to limit their calls to the sickest patients. Little Matthew remained sluggish but ate a little food and kept it down. Esther had expressed bewilderment at his illness. "I've never seen anything like it," she told Ben.

Ben felt like singing that morning as he slipped and slid his way to the barn. Bright sunshine winked in sparkling droplets of water left on leaves by melting ice and the air smelled crisp and invigorating. The few members of his family that had been infected by the Spanish flu showed every sign of recovery. Best of all, the war in France had ended. They still hadn't heard whether Holt and Esther's brother Arnold had made it safely through but at least they weren't being shot at now.

He did sing as he opened the barn doors to let the animals out to get a drink before he drove them to the pasture. Esther can't hear me, he thought. She never commented on his singing voice, but he could see that his inability to carry a tune grated on her nerves. Oh, well, the cows paid no attention and the horses didn't seem to mind although they pricked up their ears. He rubbed his horse's nose and checked Esther's mare as she drank. He expected her to foal the week before Christmas. They planned to surprise Matthew with his own pony although he suspected J. C. of letting the cat out of the bag.

It seemed strange to have so few animals to care for, but his Pa had decided to quit farming and move to Healdton. So Ben had sold his team of aging horses and planned to buy Pa's before plowtime. He wouldn't have kept anything but his saddle horse except for the fact that Esther refused to learn to drive the car and preferred driving the trap when she went visiting or to town.

As he fastened the gate of the pasture behind the animals he saw J. C. running toward him through the pecan grove. His gaze lingered with pride on that pecan grove. Just this year Jed had helped him graft some of the trees with paper shell varieties. He just could not *wait* until they produced. Over a year ago they had added a lean-to side room to Jed's cabin finishing the snug three-room log house far enough away from the main house so that Esther and Vinnie didn't have to see each other. They still didn't get along after all these years although each treated the other politely enough at family gatherings. He wished they could let bygones be bygones, but doubted it would ever happen. After all this time living with a mother and three sisters and now with a wife, he still didn't understand women.

He waited at the barn door for J. C. The boy slipped and slid as he hurried across the ice-covered hard packed yard. Out of breath, when he reached the warmth of the barn, he bent and put his hands on his knees as he labored to suck in air.

When he straightened, Ben led him to a stack of hay bales and sat beside him. He asked, "What's the big hurry this morning? And why aren't you in school?"

"I stayed home to help Mama. Papa's awful sick. Mama sent me to ask you to go for the doctor."

"But your Pa was getting well, I thought. What happened?"

J. C. began crying. He's just a little boy, Ben thought, as he put his arm around him. Let him cry it out.

J. C. snubbed and wiped his nose on his sleeve. Ben fumbled for his handkerchief and handed it to him. "Here, blow," he said. When the lad seemed able to talk, he continued, "Now tell me all about it."

"It happened the first night of the freeze," J. C. said. "Me and Pauline gathered up the cows during the day and had them in the shed. I thought Trixie was trying to have her calf then but I didn't want to bother anybody. I thought she could handle it. So I didn't say anything. Papa sent me to milk that evening and that's when I noticed how she acted. She should have been standing up, I thought, but she lay stretched out on the floor with one of the calf's hoofs showing. I went ahead and finished milking and checked her again. No hoof in sight and she looked in a bad way to me. She's a heifer, you know."

He turned and looked at Ben, his eyes beseeching. "I know," Ben said. "Heifers have a harder time. So what did you do?"

"I went and got Papa. I had to. I thought Trixie would die. He had to pull the calf. I helped him as best I could. I went and got the ropes and piece of broom handle. I watched every thing he did and, Uncle Ben, I think I could do it myself now."

Ben studied the youth. Not a vestige of resemblance to any Conover did he exhibit. He had looked exactly like his mother's father when he was born. As he approached his teens his body had begun to change so that it previewed his grown-up looks—the same square hips and sloping shoulders of his Grandfather Wade. In his mind's eye, Ben saw the same paunch settling on him in middle age. "So you think you could pull a calf all by yourself, do you?"

"Yeah. What you do, see, you find the hooves, pull them out and loop the little rope around them. Then you loop the short length of big rope in the middle and put the broom handle on the other end of the big rope so you can sit on it and use it for leverage. I might not be strong enough yet but I'm growing fast and it won't be long before I will be. Papa was too weak to pull this one by himself. I sat on his lap and we both dug in our heels and tugged until the calf came out. Yes, I think I could pull one by myself. I helped Papa pull on this one and we saved it and the cow, too."

J. C. stopped his narrative as he contemplated the next time. Ben said, "You've got it down pat, I can see. That's just the way I would do it. But tell me about your Pa getting sick. How did that happen?"

"It took a long time to pull that calf, Uncle Ben. And it was bitter cold, you remember. I thought I would freeze and Papa took a chill. I helped him to the house and he shook so hard that he had to lean against me to take a step. I built up the fire and he wrapped up in a wool jeans quilt and huddled close to the fireplace. But he never did quit shaking. Mama got up out of bed, weak as a kitten, and made a pot of strong coffee. He drank that hot coffee but it didn't warm him, either."

He began crying again. "My Papa's awful sick, Uncle Ben. Mama said he took a backset. Will you go get the doctor for him?"

"I can go right away but it might be best if I go see him first. I'll get the car started and take you home."

"No, Mama said to hurry with the doctor. I can tell she's scared to death. At first, Papa talked out of his head but now he won't say a word nor open his eyes. I'm going to run back home. I can get there before you can put water in the radiator and crank the car."

Ben hugged J. C. and let him go home. On the way to town he drove as fast as the road surface would allow. A sense of foreboding engulfed him. He knew personally of seven people who had died that fall from the flu. He had served as pallbearer for two of them, one a small child. Jed's earlier bout had been severe and, even as he seemed to have beaten the disease, Vinnie came down with it. Although he and Ma and Flora tried to help them, Ben knew that Jed had borne the brunt of her care.

When he reached Dr. Allen's house, Mrs. Allen informed him that the doctor left early that morning to make calls.

"My brother is terribly sick," Ben told her. "If you know where he might be, I'd like to try to find him."

She directed him to a rural residence unfamiliar to Ben.

"I'll try to find him but, if he comes in, please send him out to Jed's as soon as possible."

The farmhouse turned out to be easy to locate and, when Ben saw Dr. Allen's Model T in the yard, he knew he had found the doctor. Getting him to leave his patient, however, proved more difficult. At Ben's insistent urging, he agreed to follow Ben outside while Ben explained Jed's predicament.

Dr. Allen said, "I'm sorry but I'm attending this dying mother. There's no more I can do for her but I can't leave her husband and children to bear this burden alone. I'll give you some medicine for Jed, which is about all I can do for him myself when I get there. I'll come see him as soon as I leave here."

Ben had to be satisfied with the promise. He followed the doctor to his car and, taking the bottle of medicine, drove to Jed's house as fast as he could. Once there, he hurried to his brother's side and tried to hide his shock at Jed's appearance. Four days had passed since he had last seen him but Jed appeared to have aged ten years in that length of time. Dark circles around his eyes contrasted sharply with ashen skin stretched over his shrunken cheeks. In fact, his entire body seemed to have shrunk, as he lay supine in his bed scarcely making a hump under the covers.

Ben forced a cheerful tone to his voice. "Jed. Here, Buddy, I've brought you some medicine to make you feel better. I'm going to lift you up so you can take a spoonful." He put his arm under Jed, felt the bony back and shoulders and suppressed a shudder. Raising him to a sitting position, he took the spoonful of medicine J. C. handed him and forced it between Jed's lips.

Jed held the medicine in his mouth as if he didn't know what to do with it.

"Swallow, Buddy, swallow the medicine down and I'll give you a drink of water."

Jed made a valiant effort but choked when he swallowed. Ben had been ready to hold the glass of water to his lips but instead dipped the medicine spoon in the glass and poured a little water in Jed's mouth. Jed managed to swallow the water but lay back exhausted.

Vinnie and Pauline hovered behind J. C. watching Jed's bed with anxious eyes. Ben walked away from the bed and spoke softly to the waiting family. "Vinnie, where's the baby?"

"She's asleep in my bed," Pauline answered for her mother.

"Okay. Vinnie, I want you to go get some rest. I know you've been up all night and you haven't got over your sick spell yourself. Go lie down with the baby. Even if you can't go to sleep, your body will rest. Pauline, stay with your mother and take care of the baby if she wakes up. You'll be helping your Daddy by keeping Jenny quiet so he can rest. I'll stay here and look after Jed. J. C. can help me."

Ben thought they breathed a collective sigh of relief when he took over making decisions. Vinnie went to the bed and stroked Jed's forehead and left the room crying. Pauline looked at her uncle with such a woebegone expression that Ben feared she had a premonition of impending doom.

As the hands of the clock inched toward noon, Ben observed Jed's weak activity decline until he didn't move at all. Apprehension sent a cold chill up Ben's spine and he went to the window to see if he could see any sign of Dr. Allen's Ford. An hour remained until time for the next dose of medicine. Ben itched for action yet felt drawn to his brother's bedside as if his leg were tied to the bedstead.

He looked at the ten-year-old sprawled in the handmade straight chair they had brought in from the dining set. Jed had made a set of eight to match the dining table and sideboard. From the time he brought the oak planks from the sawmill through gluing them together for the wide boards, planing, making spindles, and fashioning the furniture, the process had taken longer than two years. Sturdy yet graceful, each item exhibited the care and perfection Jed demanded.

Ben hadn't prayed in years but he begged God to spare his brother. He has taken a poor lot in life, he petitioned, and made the best of it. Look at his children, at his craftsmanship, at how much I love him, he prayed. A tear brimmed over and, anxious to hide his crying from the boy, he turned away and pulled thumb and forefinger across his eyes and down his nose to wipe away any sign.

At least he could provide activity for J. C. "Son, I want you to put on your coat and run over to your grandfolks and tell them that your Daddy has taken a backset. Stop by my house on the way and tell your Aunt Esther that we don't know how long it's going to take the doctor to get here. If I'm late getting home, she will need to milk the cows. I fed and watered all the stock this morning."

After J. C. left, Ben sat by the bed and picked up Jed's limp hand, squeezed it and received no response. I wish the doctor would come, he thought. At that moment, he heard the rattle of a vehicle and the sharp pop of the exhaust as the doctor killed the engine. He started through the kitchen to open the door but found Vinnie had beaten him to it. Pauline had followed her mother and tried to go into the sickroom but Vinnie sent her back to watch the baby.

Vinnie stood at the foot of the bed while Dr. Allen examined Jed. His grave expression unchanged, he shook his head almost imperceptibly. Calling Ben aside, he said in a low voice, "I'm afraid it's bad. He may get better but he's in a coma now. I suggest you call in the family."

Ben thought they had moved out of earshot. Vinnie's scream startled him and he sped to her side. She had moved to the head of the bed and stood wringing her hands. Glancing at the patient, he saw that Jed had not moved. If the scream penetrated his unconscious mind he showed no sign of it. He put his arm around Vinnie and said, "You must get hold of yourself. You are scaring your children to death." He could have bitten his tongue to recall the poor choice of words.

Pauline came running into the bedroom sobbing. Ben knelt and put his arms around her. "Honey," he said, "I know you're scared but you need to go back to the baby. If she wakes up she'll get down off the bed and toddle in here. We all need you to be brave right now."

"I sent J. C. to tell my folks," he told the doctor. "I think I'd better go get them in the car if it's all right to leave you right now. My Pa's rheumatiz is giving him fits in this cold weather."

Vinnie put her hand on his arm to stop him. "Don't leave us," she begged. "Don't go."

The doctor intervened. "It's the best and quickest way to bring the folks here," he said. "I'm going to give you something to help you get through the afternoon. As Ben said, you need to be brave for the sake of your children."

Ben turned north at the end of the lane and drove to Flora's place. After Plez had gone to work for the Magnolia a few years ago, they had saved enough to build a new frame house. Painted white with gray trim and by far the grandest dwelling of any belonging to the Conovers; Ben thought it rivaled the grand log Wilson house. He parked in the driveway in front of the garage and entered through the side door into the dining room.

Flora came out of the kitchen to meet him drying her hands on her apron. "What's wrong?" she asked.

"It's Jed," he said. "The doctor doesn't give him much chance. He's calling in the family."

Flora blanched. "No," she said. "He's been up and about since his illness. What happened?"

"I'll tell you in the car. You need to get ready and go prepared to stay to help. It looks like Vinnie won't be much use and I don't think Ma is up to it. Matthew is still too sick for Esther to leave him and Betsy is too young. With Ida in California with her man in the Army, that just leaves you and me."

Flora pulled her apron off as Ben followed her to the kitchen. Slipping the bib strap of a clean one over her head, she said, "I just took this ham out of the oven. I'll cut off enough for Plez and the girls and take the rest with me. Oh, my land, what'll I do with Gladys? I don't want to take her with me."

At that moment, the child appeared in the doorway clutching a doll and wiping sleep from her eyes. "Mama," she said, tittering, "I laid down with my dolly to get her to sleep and I went to sleep myself."

Seeing Ben for the first time, she ran to him and threw her arms around him. Ben picked her up in his arms. To Flora, he said, "Take her to my house. Esther loves to keep her and I don't think Matthew is catching any more. Leave a note for Mary Lou and tell her to go over there when she gets in from school. Come on, I'll leave you at Jed's and take her by our house on my way to get the folks."

Ben felt relaxed by Flora's matter-of-fact way of handling things. The two of them had always worked well together. He looked with dread toward the next few hours but he thought that he and Flora could handle it together. If Jed dies…. He pushed the rest of the thought away. He can't die; I don't know what I'd do without him.

After dropping Flora at Jed's and Gladys at his own home, he brought his parents and Betsy back with him to Jed's. As they gathered around the bedside, he gestured with a jerk of his head to Dr. Allen who followed him into the kitchen.

"Has there been any change?" he asked the doctor.

"None, unless he has become weaker. He shows no signs of regaining consciousness at this time."

Ben felt a cold finger of dread hit the pit of his stomach. In a weak voice, he asked, "Do you think he's going to make it?"

"I can't answer that for sure, Ben. If you'd asked me that three weeks ago when he had such a raging fever and talked incoherently, I'd have probably said that I doubted it. He recovered from that severe illness because of his youth and strength. But this relapse struck a much different body, one worn out from fighting off that earlier bout of flu. I wish I could give you more hope. I've done everything I know to do; all we can do now is pray."

Dr. Allen left soon after to make his rounds. "I'll come back before I go to bed tonight to see about Jed," he said.

The long afternoon crawled toward darkness. Flora prepared the evening meal and called everyone to the table. Vinnie refused to leave Jed's side and shook her head when Flora suggested she bring her a piece of ham in a biscuit.

"I'll sit here with Vinnie while y'all eat," Ben said. "Bring us a cup of coffee, please."

"What do you take in yours?" he said to Vinnie.

She looked at him as if he spoke in a foreign language. Shaking her head to clear it, she said, "Just a good splash of cream," and turned her attention back to her husband.

After supper, Ben took Matt and Betsy home to tend to their evening chores. "I'll be back and pick you up in a little while," he said. "I'm going to run home and let Esther know how things are going."

Esther met him at the door. "Is Jed any better?" she asked.

He shook his head.

All the color drained from her face. Motioning him to follow her, she led him to the front room leaving the children eating at the kitchen table. Struggling with her words, she said, "Do you think there's any hope?"

Ben put his hands over his face. All day long he had put up a brave front while inwardly his spirit sank lower and lower. Sobbing, he said, "I'm afraid to hope."

Esther put her arms around him and drew his head down until it rested against her shoulder. Stroking his head and massaging his neck, she let him cry. When the fit of weeping ended, she led him to the leather couch and sat beside him. Patting his hand, she said, "Oh, my dear, my dear."

Used to Ben's deliberate way of thinking before he spoke, she waited until he began to talk. "All my life as long as I can remember we four boys were a team. Jed is two years younger than I am, true, but I don't remember a time without him. Paul is dead and we haven't heard from Buford since he left eleven years ago. Now, if I lose Jed, I'll be the only one left." Tears spilled over again and slid down his cheek.

Esther continued patting his hand while she reached in her apron pocket and handed him a handkerchief.

Wiping his eyes, he said in a strangled voice, "If I didn't have you and Matthew, I don't know what I'd do."

Matthew burst into the room and hurled himself at his father. Ben's arms closed tight around his child as he thought, Thank God that he's on the mend.

A little after midnight the doctor came back. He examined Jed and called Ben and Matt aside. "I'm afraid I have to give you a bad prognosis," he said. "He is much worse than when I left. I doubt he'll make it through the night. Now I can stay and sit with you but I've done all I can do for Jed. I feel so helpless; I wish...." His voice trailed off.

Ben looked at his father. This is his son, he thought, let him make the decision.

"Doctor," Matt said, "You've had a long, hard day and you need your sleep. Plenty of others are sick at this time. You might help some of them recover. We'll stand our watch. Speaking for myself and my family, we will be eternally grateful for all you've done." He extended his hand to the doctor.

Ben escorted Dr. Allen to his car and shook his hand before returning. He saw that his father had gathered everyone except Vinnie into the kitchen and had already told the sad news. The women wept, wiping their eyes with wet handkerchiefs. J. C., who had refused to go to bed when his sisters did, ran to Ben and threw his arms around his uncle.

As Ben hugged the boy to him, he caught Matt's attention and, raising his eyebrows and motioning with a slight movement of his head toward the bedroom, indicated rather than asked if Vinnie had been told.

Matt shook his head.

"I'll tell her," Ben said. To J. C., he said, "Stay here with your Grandpa."

Steeling himself, he went to Vinnie's side. "Vinnie."

She acted as if she hadn't heard his approach.

Putting his hand on her shoulder, he said again, "Vinnie."

She turned her head as if in a stupor and looked at him with red-rimmed, hollow eyes. Her fear seemed a palpable presence between them.

Ben said as gently as he knew how, "The doctor said..."

She screamed and flung herself across her husband. "No, no, no," she said.

Ben pulled her away as she fought him. "Vinnie, you'll make him worse." Jed hadn't moved.

Vinnie continued her loud, hiccuping wail. Flora came running to her and tried to lead her away. Vinnie resisted and collapsed back into her chair.

"I'll get a wet cloth and wash her face," Flora said. "That should calm her down."

Vinnie did quiet down after Flora washed her face. Good old Flossie, Ben thought, I can always count on her to come up with a solution.

The lean-to that he and Jed had added to the original one-room house contained the two small bedrooms. The double bed took up most of the space in the sick room along with a dresser on the dividing wall. Vinnie sat in a chair by the bed and the addition of two extra chairs filled the tiny room.

The four adults decided to take turns sitting for an hour. Ben and Lillie sat the first hour with Matt and Flora relieving them. Flora kept coffee hot and Ben soon felt his mouth draw from drinking several cups. He tried adding more cream and that helped a little. Near the end of Matt and Flora's watch, he put on his coat and went outside to walk around. The wind had laid and frost covered the ground. Sucking in a deep breath of the sharp air, he thrust his hands into his coat pockets and walked to the barn. Inside, warmth from the sleeping animals wrapped him like one of Esther's jeans quilts. Striking a match and lighting the lantern, he checked to see how Jed's animals fared. The new mother wakened, looked at him warily but didn't try to rise. He blew out the lantern and slipped back into the yard, returning to the house.

A few minutes to three, he stepped into the sick room. Flora stood with Matt. "I'm going to see if I can get Ma and Pa to settle in the big chair and little rocker and nap some," she said. "We can pull the chairs close to the fire and use Ma's shawl and the two throws she knitted for Jed and Vinnie for cover. I'll be right back."

"Any change?"

She shook her head.

Vinnie had laid her head on her crossed arms on the bed. She seemed to be sleeping but with her head turned away from him, he couldn't tell. He stood at the foot of the bed for a minute before he sat down.

True to her word, Flora returned quickly. "I got them settled," she whispered. "I was afraid they'd balk but they're both so tired." She sighed. "I hope Plez and the girls are making it all right."

"I thought Plez might come by," Ben said.

"He did come by while you were gone to take Pa home. He had Mary Lou with him and she nearly cried because she missed seeing her Grandpa. He went to your house to pick up Gladys and take the girls home for the night. You must have just missed him."

Ben chortled. "Pa'll be just as sorry he missed her," he said. "Those two have a special relationship."

Flora put on a droll expression as she said, "And he's the one who swore he would never dandle a Redskin on his knee."

Ben had started to reply when he saw Vinnie straighten up and turn to them. "He's gone," she said.

She must be mistaken, Ben thought, as he jumped up and ran to the bed. Feeling in Jed's neck for a pulse, he found none. Turning to Flora, he said, "Get me the hand mirror." When she brought it, he held it in front of Jed's face to see if his breath fogged the glass. Shaking his head, he tried again to find a pulse.

"Better get Pa and Ma," he said to Flora.

Amazed that Vinnie had remained quiet, he asked her, "Do you want to wake the kids or wait till morning?"

"Wake J. C.," she said. "Betsy's sleeping with the girls. We'll wait until daylight to get them up."

CHAPTER 16

Esther

Esther heard the kitchen door creak on its hinges and opened her eyes. Light from the eastern sky outlining the bedroom furniture showed her a promise of daylight's dawning. "Ben," she called, "is that you?"

He opened the bedroom door. "Well, it had better be, hadn't it?"

"Have you slept at all tonight?" When he shook his head, she threw back the covers on his side of the bed. "Come rest for a while. Is Jed…?"

"A little after three this morning," he said, his voice tired and dejected.

She hadn't expected the news to hit her so hard. Her heart felt like lead in her chest and she got that "all-gone" feeling in the pit of her stomach. She said nothing, not trusting her voice.

He appeared not to notice. Sitting on the side of the bed with his back to her, he tugged off a boot and let it fall. "I'm so tired that I don't want to talk about it." Plop, the other boot hit the floor. He stood and unbuttoned one side of his overalls then unhooked a suspender and shrugged out of them, pulled his shirt over his head, and slid into bed. "I have to go to town and tell the doctor and undertaker but there's no use going until the telegraph office opens. I'll send a wire to Ida. I doubt she'll be able to come."

Esther turned toward him and put her arm around him. "Don't worry about the morning work," she said. "I'll milk and feed. There's not that much to do with so few animals, anyway. You sleep until I call you for breakfast. I'll get you up in plenty of time." His steady breathing told her that her words fell on unhearing ears.

She eased her arm from him and edged off the bed to keep from waking him. Carrying her clothes, she tiptoed from the room. In the front room, she lit the gas heater and dressed. As if pulled by a puppeteer's string her eyes turned toward the picture where she had hidden Jed's note. Wrenching her gaze away, she stooped and turned off the flame and hastened from the room.

In the kitchen, she busied herself building a fire in the cook stove and grinding coffee. Faint daylight filtered into the northwest room and she could see well enough without lighting a lamp. After setting the coffeepot on the hottest part of the range, she went to Matthew's room to check on him. He slept soundly under tangled covers. When she straightened them, he sighed and settled down again.

Satisfied that Ben and Matthew were securely tucked in, she poured a cup of the hot coffee and set the pot on the back burner. She retrieved a crock of milk from the bay window and skimmed the cream into a pitcher, dropping the last spoonful into her cup. As soon as she sat to drink, her thoughts turned to Jed. She felt his arms around her as she had remembered them all week. Had it really been but one week since that night? She still couldn't believe his sudden backset and death; it seemed like a bad dream.

She jumped up from her chair catching it before it fell. Gulping the last of the coffee, she grabbed the old coat she wore for outside work and jerked it on. Without stopping to button it, she snatched the milk buckets from their pegs and ran all the way to the barn.

Soothed by the routine of scooping feed into the trough and letting one cow at a time into the milking stall, Esther cleared her mind of unwelcome thoughts as she concentrated on the job at hand. Compared with Ben's two-handed method her one-handed technique took longer. But I get more milk than he does, she thought.

The cow moved her hind leg as if to kick and Esther patted her flank with her left hand, saying, "Saugh, Pet, saugh." I need to keep her calm or she won't give down her milk, she thought. She began humming softly making up the tune as she went.

Her nerves had settled down by the time that she called Ben for breakfast. She felt certain that he had no idea of her mixed emotions. This is my husband, the father of my child, who has just lost his brother, she thought. I feel so sorry for him; he's such a good man.

"I'm going to let Matthew sleep until he wakes up," she said. "He's better but he's still not out of the woods. How's Vinnie taking it?" She set a warm plate and a cup of hot coffee in front of him.

Ben forked two sausage patties onto his plate, broke open two biscuits and covered them with gravy. "This looks good," he said. He took a big bite, washed it down with coffee, and rewarded her with a weary smile. "It is good." He ate the food on his plate without saying anything further.

Esther knew him well. He had heard her question and would answer in his own good time. Her impatience almost got the better of her but she battered it down and picked at her own breakfast, pushing it around her plate and taking a small bite now and then. When Ben took a fresh biscuit and mopped the plate clean with it, she poured fresh coffee.

"You know, Vinnie surprised me," Ben said. "She screamed like a panther when the doctor told me to call in the family. Later, when the doctor came back and said he didn't expect Jed to last the night, I thought we weren't going to get her settled down."

"That sounds just like her to me."

"Yes, but the surprising thing is that she had her head down on the bed and, when Jed died, she raised up and told us. She just said, 'He's gone' as quiet as you please. I didn't believe her but she was right. And then she made rational decisions about the children and went into the other room to let the folks mourn at Jed's bed. I don't know; she surprised me."

"It sounds like David when his and Bathsheba's child died," Esther said.

Ben served his plate with two eggs and a sausage, buttered another biscuit, and fell silent as he resumed eating his meal. When he finished, he started talking again. "What really did bother me, though," he said in a choked voice, "I overheard Ma and Pa talking. Pa said, 'Little Lillie, we just have two sons left now.' And Ma bristled up and said, 'No, Matt, we still have three sons. I know in my heart that Buford is still alive even though we haven't heard a word from him. And I'm certain sure that I'll see him again before I die.'"

Esther didn't know how to answer him but evidently he didn't expect an answer because he started bundling up for his trip to town. "I won't be gone too long," he said. "I'll ask the telegrapher to deliver Ida's answer to Mr. Wilson so he can bring it home." He shook his head. "I still can't get used to his store being closed and him working for somebody else in Healdton. Times sure have changed."

Esther tried to keep busy after Ben left, making their bed and checking on Matthew who had not awakened. She felt his forehead, found it cool and decided that this attack of vomiting had nothing to do with his recent illness. In the kitchen, she cleared the table and poured hot water from the teakettle over the dishes. As the steam rose from the dishpan, hot tears fill her eyes when she remembered tenderly covering a sleeping Jed the last time she saw him. No longer numb, she felt every nerve tingling as if from a lightning shock. Shaking, she ran from the house to the barn. Her little mare came to meet her and she buried her head in the animal's neck, sobbing.

By the time Ben returned from town she had settled into her routine and felt calm. Glad to have her storm of weeping behind her, she had spent the morning preparing food to send to the house of bereavement. Matthew got out of bed and sat at the table picking at his food. He still looks peaked, Esther thought.

She gave Ben time to tell her about the arrangements he had made before she said, "I don't think I'll try to go to the funeral."

His look almost stopped her cold. Bewilderment mingled with anger and melted into hurt.

"I don't think Matthew should be taken out when he's not well," she said. "Such a sad occasion will be hard on him; you know how much he thought of his Uncle Jed." I'm floundering around with this explanation and I know it sounds lame, she thought. "I need to stay home with him. I can keep Gladys, too, if Flora wants me to."

So they made a decision neither liked very much. When Ben started to leave to go to the service without her, he looked so dejected that Esther put her arms around him and hugged him close. "I wish I could be in two places at once," she said. "Tell all the folks that I'll be thinking about them. Take care of yourself."

The two children played together often and presented no problem. Gladys was a quiet little girl and, although Matthew had progressed in his recovery somewhat, his usual rambunctiousness had not returned. They played game after game of checkers, stopping long enough to eat the refreshments Esther served them on her tea set she had saved from her childhood.

Aside from the time spent preparing the food, Esther sat in a kitchen chair thinking of the Conovers and all their friends who were attending the funeral. Sadness filled her heart as she brought to memory each one in turn. Until now she had not allowed herself to wonder what Vinnie and the children would do without Jed. Vinnie had been estranged from her family for a long time and, as far as she knew, none of them had gone by after Jed died. I can't believe they don't know about it, Esther thought. That must be a sorry lot.

She had sung at so many funerals in her life that she knew minute by minute the progression of the service. She watched the clock and put on the coffeepot when she thought that enough time had passed for the burial to be completed. Flora, Plez, and Mary Lou arrived about the time she expected them.

"Ben has gone on to take Vinnie and the kids home," Flora said. "One of her sisters is with them and she's going to stay a day or two."

"Oh, good," Esther said. "I wondered what she would do. Were any other of her folks at the funeral?"

"Just that one sister. I think the rest of her kin has moved out of the country. It looks to me like we have Vinnie on our hands."

Esther turned away to keep the dismay she felt from showing. Deep down she concurred with Flora but she didn't want to face it. She had managed all through the years to avoid contact with Vinnie. It had been easy until she and Ben married. Afterward the two women shared a tacit agreement to stay apart. When they felt obliged to attend the same functions, they had been polite but distant. I hope Flora doesn't expect me to wrap my arms around her now, she thought.

Hoping no one noticed her discomposure, she took her largest platter from the cabinet and filled it with apricot fried pies. With her back still turned, she took them one by one from a crock and arranged them carefully.

Flora laughed. "You'd think you're getting ready to entertain the king and queen," she said. "Or maybe the whole county. That's quite a stack of pies."

Esther placed the last pie on the top center and carried the platter to the table. "I expect Ben to bring the two oldest children back with him. And I thought your folks and Betsy might come over." She could tell from Flora's raised eyebrows that she hadn't fooled her for a minute.

Ben came in then and, as Esther had predicted, brought J. C. and Pauline with him.

"Plez," Flora said, "would you go see if the folks and Betsy want to come over?"

The children went into the front room to find their cousins. Ben slumped in a dining chair while Esther poured him a cup of coffee.

"Before the folks get here," Flora said, "I think we need to discuss what Vinnie and the kids are going to do."

Ben sat up straight. "Why, they'll continue living just like they did before Jed died," he said.

Flora twisted her mouth. "On what? Winter is just coming on and I bet they don't have enough feed for their livestock. Kids their age outgrow their clothes faster than you can blink an eye."

"They won't starve," Ben said. "Jed has a couple of fattening hogs and I'm sure Vinnie has a lot of fruits and vegetables canned. They can stay right there in that house as long as they want to. I'll just have to help them out."

"Which means you'll have two households to look after," Flora said. "You know Pa won't be able to do any work with his rheumatism."

"I'll get J. C. to help. He's a big boy for his age. It's a shame but he's going to have to take on responsibility beyond his years. I don't see any help for it."

Esther heard Plez's car approaching. "I'll make clothes for the children," she said. "We'll work it out. You'll see."

True to her word, Esther sewed for all three children. I doubt they've ever had such nice clothes, she thought. I wouldn't want her to know I thought it, but Vinnie is not any hand to sew.

SPRING 1919

CHAPTER 17

Esther

On Saturday a week before Easter, Esther took Pauline to Healdton with her when she went to deliver butter and eggs. She drove the trap hitched to her mare rather than to ask Ben to take them. "We're going to stay all day," she told the child. "We'll see my customers first and then have a picnic lunch. After that we'll look at all the dry goods stores for some material to make clothes for Easter. You can pick out your own."

Pauline's eyes grew wide. It's like looking at a miniature of Jed, Esther thought. She has the same long lashes framing her deep blue eyes. Her hair is so thick it's hard to get a comb through it. Memory stabbed her heart and she grew short of breath.

Pauline said, "Aunt Essie, I've never got to pick out my own clothes in my whole life."

Esther forced the memory of Jed out of her mind with an effort. Smiling at the child, she said, "We'll see if we can find a ribbon for your hair, too."

In addition to finding just exactly the fabric that Pauline wanted, they bought three different patterns of shirting as well as material to make dresses for Esther and little Jenny. Adding the necessary notions and trim took thought and time. The clerk had totaled the ticket and announced the amount when Esther felt a tug on her arm. Looking down at Pauline, she saw disappointment on the young girl's face.

"Did we forget something?" she asked.

Pauline whispered, "My ribbon."

"Oh, yes," Esther told the clerk. "I told her she could pick out a ribbon."

The store had a varied stock of ribbon in many widths and colors. Esther feasted her eyes on pastel moires, jewel-colored grosgrains, satins and velvets in every shade of the color spectrum. She remembered how much she had loved choosing ribbons for her own hair. As a child she had a ribbon to match each frock. They cost little but afforded her such pleasure. For the last several years she had twisted her hair into a bun at the nape of her neck. I may get one for myself, she thought. I can wear it around the house.

She could see that Pauline hesitated. "Get any one you want," she told her.

Pauline's trembling finger pointed to a bolt of narrow black velvet ribbon. A stab of pain hit Esther in the pit of her stomach. It could have been the same ribbon Jed had given her the night he begged her to elope with him. No, no, no, her mind screamed.

Pauline must have sensed Esther's hesitation because she tipped her head back to look at Esther. Tugging her aunt's hand, she pulled Esther's head down until she could whisper, "Does it cost too much?"

Esther's heart went out to the child. Jed had never had an extra penny for any indulgence and now Vinnie had fewer resources. I should have been buying this child ribbons before now, she thought. "No, no," she said. "I'm sure I have enough money with me. Are you sure that is the one you want?"

"Honey, wouldn't you rather have a pretty color?" the clerk said.

But Pauline had her heart set on the black ribbon and would not be persuaded to change her mind. On the way home, she kept up a constant chatter. She didn't seem to notice that Esther's replies consisted of forced smiles and one-syllable encouragement. Esther felt as if her mind were covered by a curtain as black as the velvet ribbon. She dared not pull back that curtain to reveal the stage setting behind it.

The mare must have felt her tension through the lines. The usually docile animal pulled this way and that arching her neck and snorting. Trying to calm her, Esther said, "You're ready to get home, aren't you, girl? You've been in harness too long." She slapped the lines and the mare stretched out her gait taking them home at a fast clip.

Pauline laughed with delight. Esther's mood lightened. There's nothing like a child to keep you in the present, she thought.

Ben and Matthew met them at the barn to park the trap and unhitch the mare. Esther told Pauline she could run home through the pasture.

Pauline said, "Could I take my ribbon with me?"

Oh, yes, yes, Esther thought. I never want to see it again. She said, "Come on in the house while I unwrap the bundle. I'll get it for you."

She picked up the new ribbon. Feeling the softness of the velvet brought back vivid memories of the night Jed had proposed. The child's face dissolved into his face. Esther blinked and shook her head to clear it. She thought, am I losing my mind?

Employing all her will she got through the rest of the day. She changed into her everyday clothes, cooked supper and washed up the dishes. Afterward she caught, cleaned and stewed a chicken for Sunday dinner. While she had the range hot, she stirred up two cream pies flavoring one with coconut she had purchased that day. That'll be a nice surprise for Ben, she thought; he loves coconut pie.

Ben lugged in the wash tub for their Saturday night baths, poured in the water she had heated and added cold water. Matthew insisted that he was big enough to bathe himself and his father indulged him.

Esther left them alone while she turned down their beds for the night. It's just an ordinary Saturday night, she thought, so why do I feel like I'm walking around in a dream? She took Matthew's nightshirt back to the kitchen for him.

"Don't look, Mama," he said. Oh, my goodness, he's getting modest, she thought.

"I won't." She made a great show of turning her head when she handed the nightshirt to Ben. When he took it, she turned her back. "Tell me when I can look," she said.

She could hear Ben's chuckle and knew how much kick he got out of their exchange. When Matthew allowed her to look, she gathered him up in her arms and hugged him tight. "Now, off to bed with you. We've got a big day tomorrow. Remember it's Sunday."

"Daddy, are you going to church with us?" Matthew asked.

"Yes, I will if you want me to," Ben said.

Esther's breath caught in her throat. In all the years she had known Ben, he had never gone to church. She knew he had attended when he lived in Texas as a child. His mother and sisters were faithful now but none of the men went with them. She had prayed many times that he would become interested again but had refrained from pushing him about it. She smiled at him to let him know how much it pleased her.

However, even the seeming answer to prayer did not erase the heaviness she felt. She dried and dusted her body with powder after her bath, donned her nightgown, and turned to Ben, "I'm really tired after my shopping trip today," she said. "I think I'll go on to bed."

Knowing his disappointment that she had not waited to go to bed when he did, she wouldn't look at him. Later, when he came to bed, she pretended to be asleep. Sadness had enveloped her entire being. She lay still with her back to the light until he blew it out and crawled into bed. When she heard his steady, deep breathing that assured her he slept she rolled over onto her back. Immediately she regretted the move as tears slid from under her eyelids and ran down either side of her head into her hair.

Unable to stop the tears, she turned once again on her side pulling her pillow around her face to stifle any sound. He's dead, she thought, he really is dead. In the months since Jed's illness and death she had not allowed the thought full expression. At times it sprang into her conscious mind but she punched it back down the way she punched air out of sheets boiling in the wash pot. A sob escaped her. She tried to muffle it by pulling the pillow tighter but grief overwhelmed her. Furious at her lack of self-control, she lay rigid and smothered the sound as best she could.

Ben stirred and turned over. I've awakened him, she thought. Afraid that he would question her, she choked back the sobs and dried her eyes on the wet pillow. Taking shallow breaths, she swallowed until she thought she could speak.

But Ben lay there still and silent. As the minutes passed while he said nothing, guilt overcame her grief until all tears fled. Why doesn't he say something? I know he's awake, she thought. She threw back the covers and got up. In the kitchen she dipped water from the bucket and drank. Pouring a little water into the washpan, she splashed her face and dried it vigorously.

Back in the bedroom she turned her pillow over and lay back down. This time Ben pretended to be asleep. She stretched out on her side of the bed and, truly weary from the long day and the bout of grief, went to sleep.

Neither of them mentioned it the next day. Matthew's excitement at having his father going to church with them spilled over on them as they progressed through the busy morning. While Ben did the outside chores, Esther stirred up a batch of chicken dressing and stored it in the icebox to cook after church. The piece of ice had almost melted and she told Ben that they needed to buy more to bring home. After breakfast, she washed dishes and made beds before dressing for church. She had dressed Matthew first and Ben had a hard time keeping him from getting dirty while she dressed.

It duplicated their usual Sunday ritual except that Ben also wore his nice clothes. On past Sundays he had driven them to Graham to the little white building where they had started worshipping after the death of David Goodgion had closed the Chagris congregation. His custom had been to drive around or visit some of his friends until time to pick them up after church. But that day he parked under the shade of a tree and walked in with them. Matthew clung to his hand and danced around him all the way to the door.

Ben stopped. "Matthew, settle down or we'll stay out here," he said.

Matthew tried to stifle his exuberance with little success. As a result, Ben waved to Esther to go in ahead of them. Flora scooted over on the bench to give her room to sit but Esther shook her head. Leaning down, she whispered, "Ben came with us this morning. We'll just sit here in front of you."

When Ben and Matthew entered some of the people in front of Esther turned around, nodded and smiled in welcome. I wish they hadn't looked, she thought. It's embarrassing. The service started at once and she became absorbed in the familiar ritual. As her clear soprano soared in the spiritual songs she felt her spirits lifting. During the prayer she asked for deliverance from any more episodes of grief such as she had experienced the previous night. She felt even better after worship than she usually did.

As soon as they could, the children escaped into the warm Spring sunshine to play. The members of the congregation all knew Ben and crowded around him trying to make him feel welcome. Esther moved away with a group of other women leaving Ben visiting with the men. She could see relief on his face. His outgoing nature socialized well in all company but he always felt more comfortable with his own sex.

Esther could see on Lillie's face the joy of having her son at worship. "Come go home with us for dinner," Esther told her. "We can go by and get Mr. Conover on the way."

"I rode in with Flora," Lillie said. "Plez will be back to pick us up pretty soon. I'll go tell her I'm going with you and then see if I can round up Betsy."

The afternoon fulfilled one of Esther's girlish dreams as she entertained family after church. Ben and his father walked out to examine the fields and Esther showed Lillie and Betsy the materials she had purchased the day before.

Lillie's eyes misted. "I appreciate so much the way you've taken Jed's children under your wing," she said. "They'd never have anything new if it wasn't for you and Ben."

"I'm sure Vinnie does the best she can," Esther said. "She doesn't have any money but she works hard. She has the prettiest garden you ever saw and she wants to plant some cotton. I wouldn't have that much gumption."

"Matt and I have talked about that. I don't think she has enough space for cotton. She'd be better off raising corn to feed her stock. I wish we could help her more but, with Matt's rheumatism, it'll be all he can do to keep body and soul together for us. Holt will help, though, now that he is home and gone to work for the Carter."

The men came in then with Matthew strutting behind them stretching his legs to reach his father's footprints. "We made a deal," Ben said. "Pa and Ma have decided not to move this year. Did she tell you? But Pa feels like he can't work his place by himself this year, so we're going to go together on our crops. We'll hire Vinnie and J. C. both to work for us if they agree. I hate to ask a woman to take a man's place but Vinnie worked for her Pa like a man and I'm sure she can do it. What do y'all think?"

Lillie said, "It sounds like the best she can do for the time being. It'll be good for J. C. working with his Grandpa and you."

Esther nodded in agreement.

The following week Esther filled every spare minute with her sewing projects. She scheduled a garment a day leaving her own to the last in case she didn't finish. But the shirts for the two boys fell together and she sewed them both in one day. Being by herself so much gave her too much time to think and, although she tried to direct them otherwise, her thoughts turned to Jed and his shortened life. If a tear fell on the cotton fabric it soon dried without a trace.

After supper each night she sat with Ben while she sewed on buttons and hemmed the garment she had made that day. Except for the night *The Healdton Herald* came in the mail, Ben seemed eager to talk and Esther gladly joined in. Matthew made excited plans for his McMasters grandparents' annual Easter egg hunt the following Sunday. Esther realized how much she enjoyed these evenings beside the fire and vowed never to do anything that would destroy this companionship.

CHAPTER 18

Esther

Easter Sunday, when the McMasters family gathered after church at the home-place the men filled the first seating at the dining table while the women served. Esther secreted several chicken legs and pulley bones in the cabinet to save for the last table when the children would be served. Too many times as a child she had eaten backs and wings because all the good pieces had disap-peared.

While the children ate Arnold and his new bride hid the eggs. Esther per-suaded Beulah to stay in the kitchen and serve her own little brood. If she hides eggs, she'll show the children every one of them, she thought. Although Esther pulled all the window shades, Claude's children and Horace's boys did their best to peek. They're almost too old for egg hunting, she thought. Next year some of them will have to hide the eggs.

When Arnold called for the hunt to begin, Esther went outside to watch. Six-year-old Matthew needed no help in holding his own even with his older cousins. She observed the scattered children for awhile then sauntered down the lane. None of the other adults seemed inclined to leave their comfortable places.

At the end of the lane she turned up the road. As she neared the path to the clearing she felt drawn toward it as if pulled by a magnet. No, she thought, I told that place goodbye many years ago. I will not go back. She turned on her heel and retraced her footsteps.

However, her determination not to return to the clearing had no bearing on her desire to do that very thing. The week following the late Easter that year

- 128 -

offered little distraction in the way of necessary work. Planting beans on Good Friday had completed her garden. Working the soil around her other plants took less than a day. The past week's feverish garment making had used up the lengths of fabric she had on hand. She tried piecing quilt blocks: cutting pieces from carefully chosen prints and contrasting solids and putting them together by hand. But she soon became impatient and opened her sewing machine to stitch them faster.

The week dragged by until her Friday washday and Saturday baking. She breathed a sigh of relief when she retired Saturday night. I got through one week without yielding to temptation, she thought. I can resist the lure of the flesh if I try hard enough.

But the next morning when they passed the path to the clearing on the way to church, she said to Ben, "I think I'll go sometime this week and stay all day with Ma. I'll ask her this morning when she wants me to come. Can you look after Matthew? There are no children around for him to play with over there."

Ben agreed and so she made arrangements with her mother. Tuesday morning when Ben went to his fields she washed her dishes and gave the rest of the house a lick and a promise before she walked the mile and a half to her girlhood home. She enjoyed the fresh breeze against her skin and the cool shade of the tall trees along the roadside. It will be hot later today, she thought; I dread walking home.

At the empty McIntosh place she turned aside to smell the sweet scent of the old Seven Sisters roses she had planted when she and Ben lived there the first year they were married. Ben rented this eighty acres from Stump McIntosh still but hoped to buy it. Now that the oil checks are coming in, Esther thought, maybe it won't be too long until we can afford it. Memories of their first years of marriage crowded out daydreams of Jed and she almost turned to go home. But her mother expected her and she knew she must go face the devil of temptation that waited.

Unused to exercise, she had become winded before she reached the old house. After she rested on the steps a few minutes she drew a bucket of fresh water and drank from the well bucket, spilling water on her dress. I've got so fleshy lately, she thought, that I can't do anything without having to rest. Ben spoils me, too, not letting me work in the field.

Refreshed, she resumed the trip. When she came to the lane leading to her parent's home, she walked right on by. Disgusted with herself, nevertheless she found the path to the clearing and turned in.

The clearing had changed in the eleven years since she last saw it. It can't even be called a clearing anymore, she thought. Fallen limbs entangled in undergrowth littered the ground. Several of the trees had died leaving hollow trunks and broken branches hanging from splits. Esther began to cry. It's like my broken dreams, she thought. I wish I hadn't come.

Deciding never to come back, she turned her gaze on each tree in turn and saw near the wood lot the tree where Jed used to leave notes for her. It had grown taller and spread its limbs into places left by trees that had died but the hollow place remained within reach. Feeling like a foolish young girl, Esther picked her way to it and stretched to run her hand inside.

She heard the crackle of paper almost before she felt it. Shaken, she withdrew the folded letter and opened it with trembling fingers. She recognized Jed's handwriting; it had changed little over the years. Written with pencil on lined paper, the note showed signs of weather damage that had left it barely legible. With difficulty she read:

ॐ

"Essie,

"I don't know if you will ever see this letter but I had to write it. Ever since I held you in my arms again and kissed your sweet lips I have thought of nothing else. I know it is a long chance but someday if we are both free I want us to be together.

"Yours, Jed"

Her pounding heart alarmed her; she felt she would suffocate. The letter must have been written the day after she sat with Vinnie before he suffered his backset that night. Did he come here to leave it with the weather turning icy and a cold norther blowing? He must have. No wonder he took an uncontrollable chill that night. It's like he wrote this on his deathbed, she thought.

She read the note twice more wondering what to do with it. Her dress had no pockets. She carried her handkerchief stuffed up her sleeve but that would not do for the paper. She knew it would crinkle every time she moved if she concealed it on her person. She decided to return it to the hollow and retrieve it on her way home.

Back on the main road she walked the short distance to the lane that turned in to her parent's place. Head down, she shuffled along oblivious of singing birds or the fresh scent of the spring morning. She had memorized the short letter and repeated it over and over in her mind as she walked up the road as if in a trance.

Engrossed in her thoughts, she did not notice Beulah's young children running toward her until they grasped her hands, crying, "Aunt Essie! Aunt Essie!"

Hacked that Beulah and her brood had barged in on her planned visit, she spoke curtly to Beulah. "I didn't expect to see you here." She knew her voice sounded petulant.

"What do you mean by that remark?" Beulah said.

Esther caught her mother's forbidding look. "I could have brought Matthew along to play with your children," she said.

The mild answer seemed to satisfy both Beulah and Judith. After that, the three women enjoyed visiting except when Beulah's unruly children disturbed them. Beulah's the type that threatens and never follows through, Esther thought.

Soon after lunch, Beulah said, "Ma, I'm going for a walk if I can get away from these brats. They get on my nerves so bad I can hardly stand it. I won't be gone long; I have to get home before Timmy comes in from school."

When Beulah returned, Esther drew a bucket of fresh water so Beulah and her children could have a cool drink before they started home. After they left, Judith said, "Let's take our water and go sit on the porch swing for awhile. Maybe it will be cooler outside."

They sank gingerly onto the swing. Both women had gained weight over the winter. Once they got comfortable, Judith said, "I'm so glad Ben has started to church. What made him change his mind?"

"He decided for himself, I guess. Matthew asked him to go with us and he agreed. I've been careful all these years not to push him but I know he realized how much it meant to me. It's an answer to prayer. I can't begin to put into words how happy I am about it."

Judith patted Esther's hand. "You don't need to; I know how you feel. I regard the day when Claude and Horace left off their drinking and came back to the church as one of the happiest days of my life. I know that Ben never takes a drink or does anything else wrong as far a I can tell, but it's just better if the two of you can be agreed in this area."

Esther took her leave soon after. When she reached the main road, she looked both ways to see if anyone saw her then turned up the road and made her way to the hollow tree to retrieve Jed's note. She stretched her arm to reach the hollow and felt about inside.

The note wasn't there. It must be, she thought, standing on tiptoe and extending her fingers as far as she could. Further groping failed to encounter even a hint of paper. The tree must have a crack that the letter slipped into, she thought, looking around for something to stand on so she could see inside the hollow place. She found nothing and, after a long futile search, gave up and started home.

Pondering the note's disappearance on the way home, she began to suspect that it had not vanished into thin air. Neither had it slipped into a crack. After all, it had lain there for months with weather and animals to disturb it. Her sneaky sister must have found it and taken it with her. The fat's in the fire, she thought, I'm in for it now. She'll spread this like wild fire. I'll never be able to live it down. I'm not guilty, her heart cried, I ran away. But you wanted to stay, her conscience answered.

Grateful for the acceleration of work that time of year, Esther used busyness almost like a narcotic. She milked the cows morning and evening teaching Matthew the skill by letting him strip the last few streams of milk from each cow. She had planted a big vegetable garden and she went over every bit of it with a hoe that week. Spring salad greens and radishes furnished wilted salads for two meals a day. Unable to wait until they reached larger size, Esther grabbled one mess of new potatoes. Ben, too, worked from daylight to dark in the fields and finished chores in the barn by lantern light. Exhausted, both of them fell into bed each night to be awakened by the alarm at three o'clock to start another strenuous day.

On Saturday Esther took Matthew with her to town to deliver butter and eggs. Afterwards they bought the few staple groceries that they didn't produce on their farm along with a sack of candy for Matthew. When they got home, Ben waved from the field for them to stop and strolled down a furrow to meet them.

"Guess what?" he said. "While you were gone, Plez stopped by with his Uncle Stump. Stump wants to sell that eighty where he and Abby lived. I made arrangements to meet him tomorrow morning to see if we can make a deal. What do you think?"

"Do you have to do it tomorrow?"

Esther could tell that Ben didn't like that question.

"Yes, I do," he said. "I let my animals rest that one day a week but this time of year I must work the fields the other six days. You know how much work there is now that I promised to help Pa this year. Besides, I think Stump wants to get back to eastern Oklahoma as soon as he can. I went ahead and asked Plez to pick you and Matthew up for church when he brings Stump over."

Esther had to admit that Ben's reasoning made sense. He needed to work when he had good weather or he would get so far behind that he'd have a hard time catching up. She admired him for allowing his animals to rest one day out of seven. Although she had hoped that Ben would build a habit of church attendance by not missing a service, in a way she breathed easier knowing that he would not be there when Beulah told her that she had seen the letter.

She dreaded the encounter with Beulah that she expected on the morrow and wondered just how Beulah would drop the bomb. In her mind she replayed the awful scene at the quilting bee when Beulah danced around waving the note Jed had written her about his sudden marriage to Vinnie and spouting its contents. Beulah had grown up, married and produced four children, but behaved still as unpredictably as that twelve-year-old. Esther thought of little else during the rest of that day and through a sleepless night.

She had never wanted to miss worship so badly in her life as she did that Sunday, even on the occasion of Jed's jilting. Now she had so much more to lose: her marriage, her home, perhaps even her child. Not knowing anything about divorce, she feared the worst. She had known a few couples who separated but never one that divorced.

When they arrived at church, Esther sat in her pew with head bowed praying. Beulah didn't make it before the service started but slipped in with her children during the first song. Esther tried to put her heart into the worship but fell far short. As soon as the observance ended she made her way to Beulah's side. Perhaps they could keep the exchange just between the two of them.

Beulah handed her toddler to Esther as she always did. "I need to catch the others before they get too far away so I can go right on home," she said. "Tim's folks are coming for a visit and I promised him not to linger."

Esther followed her to her wagon not knowing what to expect but Beulah settled the baby between the two older children on the bed of the wagon and slapped the horses. Maybe her husband told her not to make a scene, Esther thought. That doesn't mean I've heard the last of it.

Gladys begged her to let Matthew go home with them for the afternoon. Flora agreed and, after making the boy change clothes, she waved them goodbye. "I'll send Ben after him this afternoon," she said.

Ben had not returned from his business appointment with Stump McIntosh. She caught two fryers and prepared them along with hot biscuits, new potatoes and cream gravy. A serving of possum grape cobbler topped with heavy cream to finish off the meal should sit just right, she thought. She hoped Ben would invite Mr. McIntosh to eat with them.

She had the meal ready to serve by two o'clock but the men had not arrived. At three she ate a cold biscuit and a piece of chicken. As the hands of the clock ground slowly through the next hour, she advanced from anticipation to anger to anxiety. Pacing from window to window, she vacillated between going to hunt Ben herself or walking to Flora's to ask Plez to drive around to look for him. Knowing that either action would be sure to embarrass Ben, she did nothing. She made herself sit in a chair and fold her hands to wait but soon jumped up to look out upon the empty driveway.

Deciding to milk early, she rounded up the cows and put them in their stalls. She had scooped feed into the trough for the second cow when Ben opened the large doors in the other end of the barn. The cow began to eat so Esther, knowing that the cow would not stand still after she finished the feed, started milking her.

Matthew ran to her while his father drove into the barn. "Mama, you didn't wait for me," he said.

"Go wash your hands and you can strip this one while I milk Pet. I'll quit early on Pet and you can finish her. How will that be?"

She saw Ben close the large doors from the outside and waited for him to come back in the barn to tell her about the land deal. But only Matthew came through the little door. She stayed with the child coaching him as he milked and finishing the job for him when his little hand grew too tired. Together they carried the three buckets of milk to the house.

She smelled the whiskey as soon as she entered the warm kitchen. Not a shadow of a doubt crossed her mind; her brothers had often reeked of the stuff. Surprise topped the list of emotions she felt. Never in the twelve years since she had first met Ben had she ever known of his taking even a sip of any alcohol. Disappointed and dismayed, she carried her buckets to the cabinet and took Matthew's bucket from him without looking in Ben's direction.

The child's excited chatter masked her silence somewhat. As soon as she could gain some semblance of control, she said over her shoulder, "Are you hungry?"

"Yes," Ben said. "I haven't had anything to eat since breakfast."

"I'll heat it up and make fresh gravy," she said. "Matthew, honey, did you eat at Aunt Flora's?"

"Mama, we had supper but I want some pie and milk."

"Wait until we're ready to eat and I'll fix you some." She poured milk into the roux of chicken fat and flour and turned up the gas flame under the pan, stirred the creamed potatoes on another burner, and slid a pan of biscuits into the hot oven. I'd better make a pot of coffee, she thought, and shuddered at the reason for it. Ben had not said another word. She looked at him out of the corner of her eye and saw that his head nodded. I'm so mad I could hit him, she thought. Instead, she dished up the reheated food and clattered it onto the table.

Ben sat up and shook his whole body to wake it. Esther set a plate and silverware for him and poured a cup of hot coffee. She turned back to the cabinet to spoon a bowl of cobbler for Matthew before taking her own seat at the table. Ben had filled his plate and started eating.

"Daddy, you forgot to return thanks!"

Shushing the child, she said, "It's all right this time. Daddy's hungry; he didn't have any dinner." In his condition, a prayer would be an abomination, she thought, as she offered a silent blessing for their food.

After she cleared the table and left the dishes to soak, she put Matthew to bed. When she came back to the kitchen, Ben had poured another cup of coffee and sat at the table drinking it. Leaving the dishes until later, she joined him.

"Tell me what happened today," she said.

"Well, we walked the place over and discussed its value back and forth. He wanted more than I thought it was worth. The land has never been plowed, you know. The grass has been grazed and mowed for hay so it's worth something but the woods are all just black jack and post oak—good for nothing but fire wood—and the house is run down and no bigger than a cabin."

"So did you make a deal or not?"

Annoyed, his eyes flashed. "Let me tell it in my own way," he said. Before he went on, he returned to gazing at the cup he kept turning in his hands. "We had gone over the house and started on the barn and sheds. In the barn he started scratching on one of the walls and, lo and behold, opened a little door I had never seen in all the time we lived there or since. He said, 'Look what I found!' and pulled out a half-gallon of moonshine. It had been there since before he left. I couldn't believe it. He said that he used to hide a supply there from the sheriff. I didn't believe it would be any good but it had a glass lid on it and tasted just fine."

Esther made a noise that caused him to look at her.

"At first, I said, 'No, thank you,' when he offered me a drink. He just took that one swig but that seemed to get the ball rolling. We dickered awhile and finally made a deal that I thought a fair price. I had to let him keep half the minerals but that's standard practice since the discovery of oil. He insisted that we drink on it and I didn't see how I could refuse."

"Ben," Esther said in as even a tone as she could muster, "you had more than one."

He had been concentrating on his coffee cup as he talked turning it in his hands until she wanted to scream and snatch it away from him. He raised his head and looked her square in the eye. "Yes, I did," he said. "And tomorrow I'm going to pick up Stump and Abby and go into Healdton to close the deal if I can borrow the money. I haven't done too much business with the bank there but I'm tired of having to mail my payments on this place to Ardmore. I like to hand a man his money and get it over with. If I know Stump, he'll want to seal the deal with another drink. I promise you I won't take but one then."

Tears filled her eyes. She wanted to beg him not to take even one. I know you've had opportunity in the last twelve years, she thought of saying. Why couldn't you tell him no? But she said nothing; she didn't trust her voice. Instead she put the tin dishpan of water over a burner to heat and then cleaned up the dishes.

Ben said, "I've had a long day and I want to go to the field for awhile in the morning while I'm waiting for the bank to open. I'm going to bed."

True to his promise Ben took only one drink the next day. He showed no aftereffects but she sniffed it on his breath. However, he didn't quit; he bought a bottle from a bootlegger and hid it in the barn. She could always tell when he had a drink although he never got drunk. They didn't discuss it. He knows how I feel about hard liquor, she thought. I don't want it anywhere around my son. But Matthew is his son, too. At least he doesn't drink in front of the boy.

They reverted to their old routine on Sunday; he drove her and Matthew to church and dropped them at the door. Matthew begged him to go in with them but he always had some excuse. She didn't try to make allowances for him. Let him squirm, she thought. The spring turned into summer and summer into fall. Matthew quit asking and the three of them settled into a pattern of life that none of them liked. Esther cried a lot when alone and Ben worked so hard that he fell asleep as soon as he hit the bed.

Ben took J. C. to work with him every day teaching him to farm. He ate with their family at noon and Esther became fonder of him each day. The boy had a quirky sense of humor and lightened the tense atmosphere that had developed between her and Ben. She could easily look at him without remembering Jed because he looked so much like his grandfather Wade.

At harvest time, every available hand worked picking cotton, even children as young as Matthew. Ben and his father weighed each sack before they dumped it in the wagon and kept a strict accounting of each individual's share, paying wages when they sold the cotton.

Vinnie and Pauline worked for Matt until they finished gathering his crop then moved to Ben's fields to finish his harvest. Esther spent each morning cooking dinner for all of them. Lillie helped her and the two of them looked after Vinnie's little Jenny.

Esther and Vinnie avoided contact as much as possible; they had never liked each other but had always been civil. Esther felt sorry for Vinnie while her sister-in-law seemed to resent her children's fondness for their aunt. Esther heaved a sigh of relief when Ben took the last load of cotton to the gin.

CHAPTER 19

Esther

The sharp rat-a-tat-tat at the front door caught Esther by surprise. Absorbed in re-reading the note Jed had sent her twelve years ago, she had not heard anyone come up. Yelling, "Just a minute," she laid the note in the frame behind the picture of her family that had been taken a few months after Beulah's birth. She had picked up the backing to replace it when Ida burst into the room. Grabbing the note, she thrust it into her apron pocket.

"Why, Ida, I didn't know you had come home," she said, rising and holding out her arms.

Ida ignored the open arms. "What are you doing?" she said in an accusing tone.

Esther's guilt caused her to hesitate. After Ben left that morning for Ardmore, she had gotten Matthew off to school and faced a rare day of solitude. She expected Ben to be gone all day making their final loan payment and paying the year's taxes on their place. Always before he had mailed the payments but today's installment marked the end of twelve long years of debt and he wanted to see the release filed with his own eyes.

As soon as Matthew left for school, her eyes had turned as if of their own volition to the picture where she had kept Jed's note hidden all these years. Determined not to indulge in maudlin memories, she had busied herself in housekeeping chores. But as she moved from room to room making beds and sweeping, she felt drawn to the picture every time she passed it. Yielding to temptation, she took it from the wall and pried up the sprigs holding the backing until she removed the cardboard and spilled the note into her lap.

Each word had been burned into her memory as indelibly as if by a branding iron but she still felt a quiver run up her spine when she read the words, "YOU are the one I love." She read the note once more and thought, he loved me as long as he lived. But this time, no tears dampened her eyes. I've cried my eyes dry this past year, she thought.

At that exact moment, Ida had knocked on the door and banged into the room. Now she repeated her question, "What are you doing?"

"Looking at the pictures I keep behind this one. I need to get some more frames so each one can be out where I can see them." She picked up the frame and shook out two more pictures. Handing them to Ida, she said, "Have you seen these?"

Ida waved them away. "I didn't come here to look at pictures," she said. "I came here to straighten you out about the way you're treating my brother. So don't try to distract me."

Esther knew from the glaring eyes and red-blotched skin that Ida intended to express her anger and nothing she said or did could stop her. She backed away until she felt her legs touch the leather seat of the duofold. Sitting down, she beckoned with her hand toward a chair inviting Ida to sit.

Ida stood over her with her hands on her hips. "I haven't been around this past year since Jed died so I didn't know how you'd been acting. But when I heard that Ben had taken to drinking again, I bullied Flora into telling me why. Seems like you've been bawling around like you're the widow instead of Vinnie. You may think you hide it but anybody who is around you can see it. And it wouldn't surprise me if half of Carter County knows it, too."

She paused for breath and Esther said, "No."

Ida hissed, "Don't try to deny it. I can see guilt written all over your face. I had a hard time believing it at first, but I knew something or somebody had hurt Ben so deep down he couldn't stand it. Nobody but you could hurt him like that. I've never seen anyone in all my life that loves a person the way Ben loves you. If I had a man like that, I'd crawl across Oklahoma on my hands and knees to lick his boots."

Ida began to pace the room, walking back and forth in front of Esther like a soldier on guard duty. "I came here to tell you a few home truths about Jed. I loved my brother and looked up to him. As a girl, I'd rather be with him than any other member of the family because of his always pulling some joke or telling some wild tale that you knew couldn't be true. Even so, you laughed and laughed until your sides ached. But he had some glaring faults and, as far as I'm concerned, he couldn't gloss them over."

Esther said, "I don't want to talk about Jed." Her voice sounded so weak in her own ears that she wondered if Ida heard.

Ida stopped pacing and stood with folded arms in front of Esther once more. "Well, I do," she said. "Over the years, you've let it slip a time or two that you didn't believe J. C. was Jed's child. You'd say, 'He sure doesn't look like a Conover.' I laughed to myself every time I heard you say something on that order. Why did you think Jed married Vinnie, then?"

"You know her Pa held a shotgun on him. You'd do what you had to do to save your own life, too."

Ida laughed. The sound sent a cold chill through Esther.

"He fathered that baby, all right," Ida said.

Esther's anger rose to the surface. "How do you know? Are you taking Vinnie's word for it?"

"I don't have to. I have Jed's own word for it."

"*You*? It's something he never discussed with his own brother Ben. And you know how close they always were. Why would he tell you?"

"He didn't tell me; I heard him say it. You see, I followed him and Vinnie that night from the dance."

"You did *what*?"

"I boiled over inside because he danced with her instead of me. Nobody else asked me to dance, so when they left I followed them. I slipped along beside the road and they never heard me. You remember the bright moonlight that night; I didn't have much trouble in the brush. I stepped on a stick once and it broke with such a loud crack that I just knew they'd caught me, but they didn't notice. They had other things on their minds.

"They walked fast at first but, then Vinnie told Jed she was pregnant—'I'm with child' she said." Ida chuckled with her mouth closed, blowing the sound out her nose like a whistle. "Jed stopped dead still; I could tell he wasn't surprised but I heard him say, 'Are you sure it's mine?' You should have heard her squeal. He took her in his arms and held her head against his shoulder until she hushed."

Esther's face blanched and her breath came in short gasps.

Ida seemed not to notice. "Then he said, 'I know it's mine.' They went on down the road then and I stood there until I thought they couldn't hear me and I skedaddled back to the party."

"But that party happened the night those killers ambushed Paul," Esther said.

"That's right."

"He couldn't have…" Esther's voice trailed off.

"Couldn't have been the father?" Ida said. "Don't bet your life on it."

"Couldn't have known. I don't believe you."

"You don't believe me because then you'd have to see Jed for what he was—a sneak. He asked you to marry him after that night. I never could understand how he thought he could get away with that. You set the wedding date for January. He must have known Vinnie would be showing by then."

A picture flashed across Esther's vision—Jed on his knees holding her hands and saying, "I don't want to wait." She buried her face in her hands.

Ida said, "Ha, you're beginning to see Jed the way other people saw him. He could wheedle his way to get most anything he wanted, especially with women. I think most men saw right through him."

Esther remembered the strange look on her father's face when she asked him once again to let her marry Jed before her eighteenth birthday. She expected a reprimand but he said, "You're both young. And Jed has a lot of growing up to do."

Ida said, "I'll say this for him, though. As far as I know, he never cheated on Vinnie once they married. I guess being raised right counts for something."

As far as you know, Esther thought. She sat with head bowed twisting a corner of her apron.

Ida's tirade seemed to have run its course. She sighed and said, "I guess I've had my say. I'll leave you to chew on this secret I've kept all these years. I just ask you to consider Ben and his feelings. I'll let myself out. Don't worry about me; I don't expect to be welcome here any longer."

After Ida left, Esther sat unmoving while unwelcome thoughts battled for admission to her mind. Ever since that fateful day of the quilting bee, Esther had fought changing her exalted opinion of Jed but she had to admit that Ida's words had the ring to truth. Several times in the past, doubts about Jed's reliability had danced around her consciousness like moths attracted to a light, but she had brushed them away. He had been a model of correctness any time they met after she and Ben married until that last night.

This past year she had hugged the scene to her heart, hearing his words and feeling his arms around her. Her own rejection of his advances had haunted her memory and set off fits of uncontrolled weeping. When Ida had said that her bawling around had been obvious to everyone, anger shot through Esther's body like lightning. But as she thought about it, shame began to replace the anger. She wondered if her grief had been that plain to see and knew for a certainty that it had. At the time, she had thought she kept it hidden even from Ben.

Disgusted by her lack of insight, she let the truth of her actions sink deep into her. Scenes from that last time she saw Jed played before her mind's eye in rapid-fire action. She remembered her feelings: apprehension that Vinnie or one of the children might catch them mixed with hunger for forbidden fruit, sympathy for Jed's physical exhaustion, temptation to succumb to his seduction. Desire and lust almost won out, she thought.

Her religious upbringing had kept her from yielding to temptation. As she retrieved her coat that night, she had thought, *Flee fornication*. I ran away then, but didn't I commit adultery in my heart? Different sins, but sin is sin. How could I have treated Ben that way?

Agitated, she jumped up and walked back and forth from one end of the room to the other. As she passed a window, she realized that the sun had shifted from east to west. It's been hours; I haven't noticed the passing of time, she thought, and shivered. It's cold in here.

Before he left that morning, Ben had built a fire in the fireplace for her. Although they had gas heat, he knew she still enjoyed a wood fire. She saw that the flames had gone out leaving gray ashes and dying embers. Tears sprang to her eyes and cascaded down her cheeks. Look how he takes care of me after the way I treated him, she thought.

As she knelt to light the gas burner, she heard the note in her pocket crinkle. Pulling it from her pocket as she ran to the fireplace, she threw it on the embers. But as the edge began to darken, she changed her mind and grabbed the tongs to fish it out. A flame licked the edge and extended a tongue that engulfed the yellowed paper. She watched as the flames died leaving the paper a blackened square. It retained its shape for a minute or two turning gray before it became one with the other ashes.

Tears dissolved to hiccuping sobs as she fell to her knees in front of the fireplace. When they subsided, she tried to understand the reasons for such wild emotions. True, Ida had hurt her feelings that morning but her feelings had been hurt in times past and she knew she would get over it. Belief that Jed had not fathered J. C. had been replaced with doubt and doubt had turned to certainty that he indeed was J. C.'s father. Shattering of girlish dreams and long-held fantasies delivered a crushing blow to her conception of herself. I've always thought I would do the right thing regardless of my personal feelings, that I could hide my own pain. Now I see that I've hurt Ben beyond measure.

That's the thing I can't stand—to have hurt him so. My good, sweet Ben, you deserve someone better than me.

The kitchen door flew open and shut with a bang. Young Matthew burst into the room shouting, "Mama, I'm hungry. What do we have to eat?" Seeing her kneeling before the fireplace, he said, "Are you building a fire? It's cold in here; turn up the heater." With that, he threw his books on the duofold and ran to warm his hands at the gas heater.

Esther got to her feet and faced the child. "Where's my hug? I haven't seen you for hours."

He turned from facing the stove and held his hands behind him. "Mama, you've been crying. What's the matter?"

"It's all right. I've been looking at some old pictures today." Enough of the truth that I don't feel guilty, she thought. "I'm over my crying spell now. I'll go to the kitchen and get you some cake and milk. You can eat it in here for once because I let the house get so cold. Now come give me a hug."

When she brought the cake and milk, she told him to play while she started a fire in the wood range. "I feel like cooking on wood this evening," she said. "When the kitchen gets warm, I'll call you and we'll work on your lessons together." She liked to practice reading, writing, and spelling with him. By the time he gets in the upper grades, she thought, I'll have a chance to get more schooling than that offered to white children here in the nineties.

She finished cooking the evening meal before sundown but Ben hadn't arrived home. "Your Daddy's late," she told Matthew. "I'd better do the milking. Go get your coat on and come with me. You can help carry the feed and then play with the barn cats until the cows need stripping."

I wonder what's keeping him so late, she thought as she gathered the milk vessels and got matches for the lantern.

She watched Matthew finish milking the last cow and had slapped her flank to send her out of the stall when she heard the old Ford chugging down the lane. Matthew raced to meet his father. Turning off the lantern before she followed him, she stepped out of the barn laden with two heavy buckets of milk. In the deep twilight outside the barn, she saw the two coming toward her, Matthew dancing around Ben talking a blue streak. Ben's slow careful step raised her hackles. He's been drinking, she thought with dismay. That's all I need after the day I've had. All the scenes of conversation that I have rehearsed this afternoon will have to wait. I want him to be stone cold sober when I tell him what I've learned about Jed. No, she corrected, what I have learned about myself.

In the kitchen, she set the milk buckets on the cabinet and lit a lamp. "We need to put gas lights in here," she said.

Ben took her remark as criticism. "I can't get everything done at once," he said.

"I didn't mean anything," she said. "It's something that would be nice in the future." This evening isn't going at all the way I planned, she thought. "Come on, supper's ready. I'll dish up and we can eat. Matthew, wash your hands."

Ben poured water into the washpan and he and Matthew washed up with much splashing and guffawing. For some reason, that irritated Esther. Keep your hat on, she told herself, that isn't the reason you're peeved. Don't take it out on the child.

She felt better after eating. "I'm sorry I don't have anything for dessert," she said. "Matty ate the last of the cake after school."

"Mama, don't call me Matty. That's a girl's name."

"And what would you want me to call you?"

"Call me Conover. That's what the boys call me at school."

"But that's too big a name for such a little boy. I know what, I'll call you Connie," she teased.

Ben looked from mother to son grinning as he enjoyed the interchange. "Come on, Son, before she thinks up some more girl's names for you. We men will go play a game of checkers while Mama finishes up the woman's work. Then it's off to bed for a big school boy."

Matthew's scowl disappeared as he jumped up from the table and ran ahead of Ben to the front room. Ben smiled at Esther and repeated his usual after din-ner "Good meal, Essie" before he followed.

Esther considered talking to Ben that evening. I want to get it said before I change my mind, she thought. Then, stiffening her back, she determined not to change her mind. I've always acted on my convictions and now that I'm convinced that I have been so wrong all these years, I'll put it right at the first chance. But I'll set the scene tomorrow. I'll fix his favorite dinner and tell him then. And when he says 'Good meal, Essie' I'll know that it isn't just politeness that makes him say it.

Esther washed Matthew beside the warm kitchen range giving special atten-tion to his feet and told him to change into a flannel nightshirt. "Run kiss your Daddy good night and crawl between the blankets before your feet get cold," she told him. He ran to do her bidding while she threw out the water and cleaned the wash pan. Then she blew out the light, followed him to his bedroom and tucked him in by the dim glow from the gaslight sconces in the front room.

When his breathing indicated that he slept, she returned to her chair beside Ben's under the gaslight. He seemed engrossed in reading his newspaper so she lifted her workbasket from beside her chair and set it in her lap. Rummaging through it, she found her thimble and picked up the quilt block she had begun. Itching to talk, nevertheless she hesitated disturbing him. Although his reading ability outshone her own, he had to concentrate to make sense of the things he read.

Before long, he laid the paper aside. "I picked up this *Ardmoreite* in town today," he said. "Somehow I can't seem to concentrate on it tonight."

"*The Healdton Herald* came in the mail today," Esther said. "Maybe you'd rather read it."

"No, I think I'm too tired to read. It's been a long day."

"You were late getting in. Did you have any trouble?"

"No, I came by Pa's on the way home. Ida is home on a visit from California. You won't believe what she's done."

Well, I know one thing she's done, Esther thought, and waited for him to go on.

"You know that hotel in Healdton where Ida cooked before she married. She took Vinnie there today and got her a job."

Esther dropped the quilt block into the workbasket and said, "No!"

"Yep, she did. She borrowed Holt's car. You know, I don't know another woman besides Ida who knows how to drive. So she borrowed Holt's car—he rode to work with Plez today. Of course, Holt didn't know Ida borrowed his car until he got home from work. He leaves the key in it like everybody else does. So she went and got Vinnie and took her in to see the woman who runs the hotel and she hired her to clean rooms and wash dishes and sheets and table-cloths and things. I don't know why none of the rest of us ever thought of something like that for Vinnie. She needs a job as bad as anyone I know, but she is too backward to go look for one herself."

He chuckled while Esther tried to think of something to say. When she didn't reply, he said, "That Ida can sure stir things up."

More than you know, Esther thought. She has been extra busy today.

"Did you know she is here?" Ben said. "She got in yesterday."

"Yes, she came by this morning." Esther wondered if she sounded short, but Ben didn't seem to notice.

"They are giving Vinnie two rooms at the hotel and meals for her and the kids and a little something a month. Ida didn't say how much. I don't know if she knows; I figure it's Vinnie's business."

Esther sucked in her breath. "Ben," she said, "this means that J. C. and Pauline will be going to school in town. How are we going to tell Matty? He thinks the sun rises and sets in J. C. He'll miss him so much."

Ben pondered the problem. When he spoke, he had reached his solution. "The kids will be going to school tomorrow to get their books and tell the teacher they're moving. We'll let J. C. tell Matthew; it's his news. If his Mama doesn't need him, we can let J. C. come out here on Saturdays and take him home on Sunday. That is, if he won't be too much trouble for you."

Esther shook her head. She liked the boy. "It'll be just fine for him to come. Maybe that will mollify Matty."

"I think I'll use him on the farm next summer, too. He's big for his age and a good worker. He needs a man to train him. Living in town without enough to do can be bad for a boy."

"That sounds like a good idea to me. I know I'd be glad to have someone like you help my boy in the same circumstances." Esther breathed a short prayer that she would never face a life without Ben. Now that she saw what a ninny she had been, she *must* have the chance to make it up to him.

"So, anyway," Ben said, "we are going to move her tomorrow. Ma and Flora and Ida will help her pack and we'll load her things on Pa's wagon and take them in to town. She won't need all the furniture she's got so she's going to leave it in the house until she decides what to do with it. I think she'll sell some of it. She needs the money."

"She should get a pretty penny for the pieces Jed made. They are works of art," Esther said.

"Yes. I hope some of his folks can buy part of them, at least. It'd be nice to keep them in the family." He rose, stretched and yawned. "I think I'll turn in early. I've had a tiring day and tomorrow will be another busy one. Oh, we decided to take our lunch with us so eating won't slow us down. Fix me one when you get Matthew's ready in the morning, will you?"

"I'm going to cut out enough pieces for another block or two before I go to bed. You know, I could keep Flora's and Vinnie's little girls tomorrow so they won't be in the way."

Ben leaned over and kissed her on the forehead. She lifted her face wishing he would kiss her on the lips but the goodnight forehead kiss had become ritual. "That's sweet of you, Essie. That'll be a big help, I know."

It looks like I'll have to stew in my own juice, she thought. Serves me right for the way I've treated him all these years. A scrap of scripture came to her mind—*the body without the spirit is dead*—and her eyes filled with tears. That's what I've given Ben, she thought, my body but not my spirit. I hope he won't hold it against me.

Esther

The next day Esther got up earlier than usual and fixed extra sausage, eggs, and biscuits for the two lunches she packed. She put back a pan of biscuits to become sour planning to bake them at noon to serve her and the two little girls. For breakfast, she added a big bowl of cream gravy and set out butter and sand plum jelly. All three of them drank coffee with their meal but Matthew's cup contained more cream than coffee.

After her men left, she checked a big bucket of water she had set on the burner to heat and found that it had started to steam. Time to catch that old hen, she thought. I've been saving her for a special occasion. As the chickens scratched and gobbled up the grain she fed them, she took a long, heavy wire with a crook at the end and hooked the hen's leg. Drawing the squawking creature to her, she wrung her neck with a quick snap of the wrist. The other chickens scattered as the hen flopped and then lay still on the ground.

Esther carried the big bucket of scalding water to the yard and, holding the hen by her legs, dipped her to loosen her feathers. The pungent odor almost gagged her and she hastened to pluck the big feathers dropping them into another bucket for later disposal. Some people use chicken feathers to stuff pillows, she thought, but I can't stand them. I don't waste much but I don't consider throwing out chicken feathers to be wasteful.

Next, she slit the abdominal cavity and, saving the liver and gizzard, she discarded the rest. Slitting the gizzard, she skinned the lining. After dumping the hot water, she dropped the hen in the bucket and carried it to the kitchen sink. This year Ben had run plumbing from the well and installed a hand pump so that she had water right in the house. He hired a tinsmith to make a sink and ran a drain line for the gray water. It's just another instance of his thoughtfulness, she thought. I have taken this good man for granted too long. I'll never, never repay him.

As she stood at the sink washing the hen thoroughly, she glanced out the window and saw Ben leading two little girls across the pecan grove. He stopped and placed the hands of Gladys Wilson and Jenny Conover together. The children proceeded toward the house with Ben watching.

Esther shook water from the hen and carried it to the gas stove. She had lighted a top burner before she washed the chicken, and now she passed it back and forth in the flame singeing off the pinfeathers. After turning off the gas, she salted the hen and placed it in the pan of water she had heating on the wood stove. Ben laughs at me for using this old stove, but I can control the temperature better, she thought. This lease gas pressure fluctuates so much I have to watch it every minute.

Five-year-old Gladys pushed the kitchen door open and led her two-year-old cousin into the room. Grabbing her nose, she said, "Peuw-wee, Aunt Esther, something stinks."

Jenny clamped her nostrils with her tiny fingers and said, "Poo-wee, Aunt Etter."

Esther picked up the little one and hugged her. She looks as much like her mother as J. C. looks like his Grandpa Wade, she thought. But she has a sweet disposition; you can't help loving her. Setting Jenny down, she opened her arms to Gladys. Quiet by nature, black-haired, brown-eyed Gladys always waited for an invitation. She's the image of Polly, Esther thought. I always think that, if Polly had married and had her own children, they would look like this one.

She spread an old quilt on the clean plank floor and gave the girls rag dolls to play with. If I ever have a girl of my own, she thought, she will have plenty of playthings. She saw Gladys struggle with her natural reticence and overcome it to ask, "Can we play with your tea set, please, Aunt Esther?"

"We'll save that until midafternoon," Esther said. "That's the proper time to have tea." They're good little girls, she thought, no trouble to keep.

She scooted the chicken pot to a cooler spot on the range so that it bubbled in a slow simmer. She sang as she collected the ingredients to make an apple pie. I'm so glad to have all the flour I want again, she thought remembering wartime shortage. I can have hot rolls, dumplings, and a pie all at one meal.

After the noon meal, she told the girls that she would open out the duofold so they could take a nap. "When you wake up," she told them, "I'll have a surprise for you."

Gladys didn't like the idea. "I'm too big to take a nap," she said. "I'm going on six."

Taking her on her lap, Esther whispered in her ear, "Jenny needs a nap. Look how she's yawning. But she won't lie down without you. So I want you to lie down with her until she goes to sleep. Then you can get up."

Jenny pulled on Esther's skirt. "Tell me secret," she said.

Laughing, Esther set Gladys down and picked Jenny up. Rocking her back and forth, she whispered, "Your doll babies need a nap. Take them to bed with you and get them to sleep."

"Aw wight," Jenny climbed down obediently and took her doll to bed.

Esther covered the girls and dolls with a quilt and told them to stay quiet while she went to the bedroom for a little while. Once there, she got a length of white outing flannel from a bureau drawer and unfolded it on the bed. She had bought enough to make two gowns but instead she cut out one for herself and a nightshirt for Ben. When she carried the fabric to the front room where she kept her sewing machine, she saw that both children had fallen asleep.

At first, she feared that the bump-thump of the treadle would waken the sleepers, but neither starting nor stopping affected them. Ben's shirt fell together fast. She seamed the shoulders, put cuffs on the sleeves and sewed them in, faced the neck and placket, then stitched the three pieces together. A quick shirttail hem left the garment finished except for handwork of buttons and buttonholes. Her gown took longer because she had fleshed out so much here of late, but the entire project still required less than three hours.

She stopped before the children stirred and went to the kitchen to bake the treats she had promised them. Late that morning she had mixed a large batch of yeast dough and set it to rise. Having punched it down midway of the sewing project, she had it ready to knead and bake. Separating out a third of the dough, she sprinkled it with sugar and worked it adding more sugar until she had a sweet base for her famous butter rolls. She rolled it out, spread it generously with softened butter and sprinkled more sugar on top. Before she rolled it, she cut out a small square that she folded into a tight circle and then cut into six pieces and put into a pie pan. Just as she slid the pan into the oven, she heard the little girls padding barefoot into the kitchen.

"Go put on your shoes and then wash your hands," she said. "I'll get out the tea set and you can get ready for your party." She spread a quilt out of her way near the outside door and laid her clean breadboard in the center. When she handed Gladys an embroidered cup towel and two diminutive napkins she had cut from scraps of the new outing, the child laid the pretend table.

Esther enjoyed seeing the children play with her old tea set. She remembered her fifth birthday when she received the set. Her parents had settled in Indian Territory with their children over a year before but, when Christmas came and went without gifts from her grandparents back in Arkansas, she cried and cried. As it turned out, they had misjudged the vagaries of the mail delivery and the package arrived a few days after Christmas. They had sent toys to her brothers but a new dress each to her and baby Beulah. She tried to act pleased but a tear rolled down her cheek instead.

When she went to the table on the morning of her birthday, imagine her surprise and delight to find her place set with a five-inch plate and three-inch saucer and cup big enough to hold several sips of milk. Her mother had filled the squatty teapot with milk and one of the remaining plates with miniature biscuits. The entire four-serving set was made of heavy white crockery with a blue rim around each piece.

She had taken particular care with the set during her childhood and Ma had never let harum-scarum Beulah touch it. After she grew up, Esther had allowed children to play with the sturdy toy but always under her watchful eye. She wanted to save the dishes in case she ever had little girls of her own.

While Gladys set the table and poured imaginary tea from the teapot into cups, Esther prepared a large pan of the remaining butter rolls and popped them into the oven. The small rolls had turned a golden brown so she asked the children for one of the extra plates and put them on it to cool a little. Then she filled the teapot with milk and called Gladys to her. "You'll be the hostess and do all the serving because Jenny's little hands might spill the tea," she said.

All day long anxiety had gnawed at her but she had held it at bay by keeping busy. She had rehearsed over and over the speech she planned to make to Ben. She knew what she wanted to say but wasn't sure of the best way to approach it. If they could be alone, she thought, things would work out better. Matthew could be a chatterbox and, with no school tomorrow, he would want to stay up late.

She tucked the last roll into the pan and set one pan near the stove to rise fast while she placed the other farther from the heat. She planned to take the first batch to Vinnie for their supper and bake the other when Ben got home.

The kitchen door opened and slammed back against the wall as Matthew almost ran over the tea table in his rush. "Mama, Mama, did you know J. C. is moving to Healdton?"

J. C. and Pauline followed him with Flora's Mary Lou running in a few minutes later. The tea party ended in a scattering of dishes and Mary Lou hurried to gather them up before someone stepped on them. Jenny ran to Pauline chattering and excited but she had lapsed into baby talk and Esther couldn't understand her.

"All you children sit down at the table and have some butter rolls and milk while you tell me all about it," Esther said.

"Mama, can I stay all night with J. C.? He's moving tomorrow and I won't get to see him any more." Matthew started crying.

"Sure, you'll see him," Esther said. "Now hush and eat your butter roll while it's still hot."

Matthew snubbed and pleaded, "Let me stay all night tonight, please."

"Please let him, Aunt Essie," J. C. said around a mouthful of butter roll. "I know Mama won't care."

It seemed like answer to prayer but Esther said, "We'll have to see what his Daddy says."

Pauline said, "Mama told me to bring Jenny home when I got in from school. Has she had a nap?"

Entranced as always by the child's marked resemblance to Jed, Esther merely nodded. It amazes me that a girl can look so feminine and yet take after her father so much, she thought. Funny how it doesn't make my heart do a flip-flop anymore when I look at her. I see her for what she is—a beautiful child—rather than a reminder of Jed.

When the children finished their after-school snacks, she sent them all to Vinnie's. Managing not to hug Matthew in front of them, she nevertheless failed to hold back an admonition. "Mind your Daddy, now."

While the first pan of hot rolls baked, she sewed on buttons and finished buttonholes on the sleep garments. She carried them to the bedroom she and Ben shared and arranged them on the bed. First she laid them across the bed, then moved them so that they lay lengthwise with shoulders just touching the pillows. She considered putting the sleeves hugging each other but instead settled on placing the cuffs touching as if holding hands. I hope he doesn't think I'm silly, she thought.

When the rolls were brown, she took them from the oven and slipped them, pan and all, into an old clean pillowcase. Wrapping it in a quilt to keep it warm, she carried it to the workers along with a pail of butter.

Ben saw her coming and hurried to meet her. Relieving her of her burden, he said, "We were just fixing to quit. We got the wagon loaded except for the few things they'll need for the night, but it's too late to make the trip to town. I'm going to drive the wagon into their barn and use our new young horses to replace Pa's mules tomorrow." He smiled at her. "This bread sure smells good."

"I thought there'd be plenty for everybody to have a bun apiece and enough left for their supper. Did Matthew ask you if he could stay all night here?"

"Yes. I haven't told him yes or no yet. What do you want him to do?"

"I think it'd be all right."

When they set the bread and butter on Vinnie's table, Esther refused to take a roll, saying, "I have another pan ready to bake for our supper."

Ben said, "I'll go put the wagon up, then, and we can walk home together."

Esther folded the quilt and pillowcase to take home. She visited with the other women until she saw Ben leave the barn. "Well, it looks like he's ready to go," she said. "I'll bid you goodbye. Matthew, you mind Vinnie, you hear."

At home, she cooked their meal while Ben took care of the evening chores. Earlier in the day, she had transferred the hen to a platter to cool, then cut it into pieces. After she got a hot fire going in the range, she pulled the pot of broth over it to heat while she made dumplings. She dumped a quart of green beans into a stewpan and set it on the stovetop with the broth pot. For the dumplings, she made a rich biscuit dough adding a spoon of butter "for the pot", rolled it thin, and cut it into strips. Pulling pieces from each strip, she dropped them one at a time into the heaviest boil in the pot. Once all the dumplings had been added she covered the pot and moved it to a cooler spot on the range to simmer. She seasoned the beans with sugar and meat grease and slid the pan of rolls into the oven.

Satisfied that she had the food preparation well underway, she spread her best drawnwork linen cloth on the table. She found two place settings that had no chips and set them and silverware on opposite sides of the table along with napkins that matched the tablecloth. It's not our usual places, she thought, but I don't want anything about tonight to be ordinary. I want us to face each other like a romantic couple.

She had just put the percolator on the stove and uncovered the dumplings when Ben came in from the barn. He sniffed appreciatively and said, "Have I missed something? Is this some special occasion?"

This may be the most important night of my life, she thought, and swallowed hard to still the butterflies in her stomach. "When you and I eat a meal alone, just the two of us, that's a special occasion," she said. "Can you remember how long it's been?"

Ben shook his head. "Where do you want me to sit?"

"I'll sit nearest the stove so I can reach the hot rolls and coffee easier." I sound like Ben is company, she thought. I'm not sure that's what I want to do.

"Maybe I should put on my suit," he said. "I didn't expect it to be so fancy."

She giggled. "It's not that fancy," she said. "I still have my apron on. But it does bring back memories of when we were first married. I don't remember any time when we were sparking that we got to eat alone."

"Maybe not," Ben said, "but Plez and Flora left us alone right after our picnic that Fourth of July. Remember?"

"I was so plagued; I thought you might think that Flora and I had made it up."

"You showed it, too." Ben's eyes got that teasing look she hadn't seen in several months. "You jumped up and started to run off."

Esther laughed outright. "And you leaned over to stop me and caught my foot. I tripped on my skirt and fell right into the middle of the tablecloth. I had leftover food all over my dress; I thought I'd have to go home."

She finished dishing up the food and sat down opposite Ben. "Would you like to offer thanks?" she said.

"No, you go ahead." The ritual question and answer brought her back to the present. She had always considered it the man's place to lead prayer but she found it impossible to eat without first asking a blessing for the food.

"Butter your bread first while it's hot," she said.

He buttered his rolls and passed the butter to her. Silently she broke open her two rolls and slathered them with butter. Then she bowed her head and asked a blessing on their meal.

Their companionable banter vanished. It's like reality sat on it and held it down, she thought. Without Matthew there to keep up a steady stream of conversation, they ate the meal in silence except for comments about the food. We've come to this, Esther thought. It's all my fault; I've withheld my love for so long. I didn't even notice the damage I've done, she thought, and almost choked on a bite of bread.

Ben scraped back his chair and rose, laying his fancy napkin beside his wiped-clean plate. "Good meal, Essie," he said.

"Thank you, Ben," she said. "You go on in the front room while I clean up the kitchen. If you're not too tired, could you build a fire in the fireplace?"

He smiled then. "I'm not too tired. By the time you get through we'll have a roaring fire."

Maybe the smile is a good sign, she thought. It doesn't matter; I've made up my mind to say my piece tonight. If she didn't, the position of the nightclothes would require some explaining. She had deliberately laid that obstacle to bolster her resolve, but her apprehension had risen to such a high point that she longed for relief. She must speak her whole heart and face the consequences. He might reject her—might say, "It's too little, too late." He might not believe her. Worst of all, he might be indifferent.

She dried her hands and hung the cuptowel on the rack, pulled her apron off and looped the neck strip over its hook, and blew out the light. At the door she stopped and took a deep breath, smoothed her hair with both hands, and gripped the knob. Standing erect and as tall as her short stature allowed, she strode into the front room.

Ben looked up from the newspaper. "The fire is catching on," he said. "I'll add a bigger log in a minute."

"It's fine," she said holding her hands toward it to feel the warmth. She turned to face him but he had gone back to his paper. Moving to her chair near his under the gaslight sconce, she picked up her sewing basket. No, she thought, I won't sew tonight. She moved to the duofold so that she sat opposite him.

He laid the paper aside and went out to the porch to bring in an armful of logs. Dropping the logs into the wood box, he picked out one of them and added it to the fire. Using the tongs, he positioned it to his satisfaction and raked coals against it. A tongue of flame leaped up and caressed the bark. Switching to the poker, Ben pushed the log atop the smaller sticks of blazing wood. Smoke curled around the new log and rose up the chimney. Ben stood the poker in its rack, returned to his chair and picked up his newspaper.

"Ben," Esther said. Her voice sounded weak to her with a little croak in it.

He laid the paper in his lap and gave her his attention but said nothing.

"Ben," she said again, "could we just talk tonight? It isn't often that we have the evening to ourselves, just the two of us."

"After Matthew goes to bed, it's just the two of us every night," he said, trying to hide his teasing smile but not succeeding very well.

"It's not the same somehow. I don't feel like having a serious conversation when he might call out and interrupt at any minute."

The teasing light returned to his eyes. "You want to have a serious conversation tonight?"

"In a way. I want to talk about when we were young and reminisce the way we did before supper."

His expression softened but his eyes took on the wary look of a new puppy in strange surroundings. He waited for her to go on.

"That day when I fell in the leftovers," she said, "I remember you took over and kept me from striking out home."

"I felt sorry for you but I wanted you to stay around, too."

"You went and got Flora and she took me to her buggy and sponged off my dress. Then you took me for a walk in the sunshine for it to dry. I didn't know until we got back that you missed your ballgame."

"But we played horseshoes, remember. I took you as a partner so my strength would overcome your being so little. I thought you might could pitch a horseshoe ten or fifteen feet. I didn't know you were an expert. I just hollered when you knocked Plez' leaner a-winding."

"I'd played all my life after I was big enough. Pa took me as a partner against Claude and Horace. He worked with me and taught me all the fine points."

"Remember I asked you to walk out with me," Ben said and chuckled. "We literally walked out together earlier in the day as a necessity, I thought."

"So many people misinterpreted that walk. They expected us to be a couple from then on."

"I recollect I had a hard time talking you into it but we *were* a couple from then on." Ben moved to the couch to sit by her and picked up her hand. "Remember the night you proposed to me?"

Esther laughed. "I did not. You started it."

"But you accepted."

Esther felt her facial muscles tighten. This is the opening I have been looking for, she thought, but I'm scared. What will I do if he rejects me? "It shames me to remember that night," she said.

He dropped her cold hand as if he felt the wintry blast that had cooled it. She hastened to explain. "I don't mean anything you did or said. I always say the wrong thing. Let me start from the beginning."

He looked puzzled so she hurried on.

"Hear me out, please. I've been doing some soul searching the last couple of days. Oh, Ben, I can see so many things I've done wrong." She sought his eye contact to plead with him but he looked at his own hands. "Go back to the night you proposed. You asked me to tell you I loved you and I said I couldn't tell a lie."

He got up, then, and walked to the fire extending his hands as if to warm them.

"You said it didn't matter; you loved me enough for both of us. But it wasn't enough." He hunched his shoulders and hung his head. I haven't said it right, she thought, I've hurt him again.

"Let me start over again," she said. "Ben, please look at me and let me try to explain."

He turned toward her at her urging and looked her in the eye. It's the way he is, she thought, honest and above board. "I don't want to hurt you," she said, "but I'm afraid what I'm going to say will hurt you. I've tried to think of any other way but I can't. I hate to speak ill of the dead but I must bring Jed's name into it."

He made a move as if to stop her but she shook her head.

"Ben, I was a young and foolish girl when I met Jed. You know everybody loved to be around him: so fun loving and hard working and church going and handsome to boot. We fell hard for each other. But you know that, too. I thought at the time that he fulfilled all my dreams. Then, when he married Vinnie, I thought she had trapped him—that he had nothing to do with her pregnancy."

She couldn't stand the hurt in his eyes. Bowing her head, she breathed, "God forgive me, I believed it all these years."

He said in a choking voice, "Have you changed your mind?"

"Yes, I have." She stiffened her back and sniffed back her tears. Looking him in the eye again, she said, "I've gone over it all in my mind. I've faced all the little incidents that I kept locked away from my consciousness. I didn't believe he knew about the child when he begged me to marry him right away. He didn't want to wait until my eighteenth birthday. He kept after me to beg Pa to sign for me. I went to Pa more than once and he refused. He just said, 'Jed's too young' but I thought he had something more against Jed."

Ben's expression changed subtly. He knew about this all along, she thought, and never mentioned it.

"There's no excuse for me to have been so gullible all these years. Like a silly schoolgirl I hung onto my dreams. When J. C. came along without a scintilla of Conover resemblance, I told myself, *see there, it isn't his baby*. Then Jed buckled down and made the best of a bad situation I thought he didn't deserve. And when he died…"

Ben shook his head violently. "No," he said, "say no more."

"I have to, Ben. I have to apologize. I've done you a great wrong. I held on to my fantasies and thought I hid it; I thought I was a good wife to you." She snorted and said in disgust, "I didn't know the meaning of the word. I see the difference now. I guess I've grown up; it's taken me a long time. You're the honest, truthful man I thought your brother to be. There's not an underhanded bone in your body. In spite of Jed's so-called Christianity, he didn't mind shading things to his own advantage. I guess what I'm trying to say is that I let his beguiling ways enchant me until I got charm confused with character. I see now that you're the one who is a truly honorable man."

"But you said my love wasn't good enough for you," Ben said. "What about that?"

She rose and took his hand. "Come with me," she said and led him to their bedroom.

Holding hands, she and Ben stood looking at the nightclothes. Still he said not a word.

I have to say it right this time, she thought. "Ben, I tried to tell you with this gown and nightshirt that I want us to go hand in hand from now on."

He turned to face her, disbelief and hope fighting for the upper hand.

"What I'm trying to say in my bumbling way," she said, "is, Benjamin Watson Conover, I love you."

He dropped her hand. "Essie," he said, "wait right here. I'll be right back."

Esther heard the kitchen door close. Fear gripped her heart as she wondered if he had gone to the barn to take a drink. If he has, she thought, it's more than I can bear. We can never understand each other then.

She heard the back door open and close again and Ben returned to her side. "Esther," he said, "you've tried to explain away all the years of hurt and misunderstanding. I could accept it and welcome it except for this." He handed her a yellowed sheet of paper. She instantly recognized the note Jed had written her just before he died. "Explain this away."

"Where did you get this?"

"In the hollow tree where Jed left it. That day when you went to stay all day with your Ma I had to go to the blacksmith. Matthew went with me and, while we were still a long way down the road on the way back, we saw you come out of the trail and turn in at your folk's lane. Matthew hollered as loud as he could but you had your head down and never heard him. I had my suspicions so I took him to Flora's and came back. That's when I found the note and took it with me."

"I can explain it," she said in the voice of a little child. "What do you want me to say?"

"I want to know when you went behind my back with my brother. How long did this go on?"

"It didn't go on at all, not like you mean." Seeing the unbelief in his eyes, she hastened to explain. "I've always been a faithful wife to you, Ben. I don't care what the letter says. What he refers to in the note all happened the night I sat up with Vinnie. In Jed's weakened state, he fell asleep in a chair by the fire. I went to cover him with a quilt and he woke up. He appeared to be dreaming when he took my hands and stood up and put his arms around me. I didn't think anything about it—he was so tired—until he kissed me. I realized then that he still had feelings for me. I pulled away and I, I came home."

Ben's expression hadn't changed. Esther thought, It's not good enough; he doesn't believe me.

"I never saw him again." Her voice broke and tears streamed down her face. She covered her face with her hands. When her fit of weeping ceased, she looked Ben once again in the eyes. "He must have put the note in the tree the next day because he took a backset the next night. I found it that morning when I went to see Ma."

She could see belief softening the expression on his face but his eyes remained wary. He put his arms around her but she jerked away. "No," she said, "No, I want to get everything out in the open between us. Then, if you don't want me, I'll leave. It's true; I never cheated on you physically. But, Ben, all those years I kept a corner in my heart for a memory of Jed. And when he died it seemed like he left a chapter in my life unfinished. But everything that I told you earlier tonight is true. I have come to realize that you're twice the man he ever could have been. I've cheated you all these years while acting the part of a good wife." Once again she snorted her disgust and repeated, "I didn't know the meaning of the word." All the while she had been talking she had forced herself to keep her eyes fastened on him. She wanted to hang her head in shame but she *had* to see how he reacted. Her life depended on it.

Ben's expression softened and his gray eyes reminded her of a soft rain that broke a long drought. He put his arms around her again and pulled her head against his shoulder. "Say it again," he said.

"I didn't know…"

He cut her off. "No, tell me how you feel about me now."

"I love you, Ben, I love you with all my heart."

"Memorize that," he said. "You're going to have to repeat it every day for the rest of your life."

Epilogue 1945

Chris Conover edged his way through the crowd after his buddies disappeared with the girls they had picked up on the midway. When they spied the two girls, the three sailors had flipped coins for the right to approach them and he had come up odd man out. Maybe he had lost and maybe not, he thought. At home, he had no trouble attracting the opposite sex. He saw his distorted resemblance in a wavy mirror under the sign proclaiming "Fun House" and bent his knees and stooped until his reflection looked almost natural. Adjusting his summer issue white Navy hat at a jauntier angle, he checked his neckerchief and decided it would do.

In the crazy mirror the image of an old man sweeping cigarette butts into a dustpan swam into his view. He looked so much like Uncle Ben that Chris whirled to stare at him. But the man had turned away from him with his head no longer in sight.

Chris chided himself for his lack of sophistication. Small town boy this far from home on his first pass since basic wanted to see someone he knew. With most of the young men in service—he had enlisted at seventeen shortly before he finished high school—these old geezers had to fill in. The war in Europe had ended last month, but no telling how long the fighting in the Pacific would go on. Chris just hoped it would last long enough for him to see some action.

His gaze kept returning to the old man and the feeling persisted that he had seen him before. He went up to a stand and bought a Coke, sat down at one of the outside tables to sip it and have a cigarette. Then the fellow faced him full on and he almost shouted "Uncle Ben" before he caught himself. It couldn't be; Uncle Ben couldn't have traveled so far from the farm with wartime restrictions on gasoline and the trains crowded with troops. But this guy looked enough like him to be his brother.

Chris dropped the cigarette he had just lighted and kicked it between him and the worker. The old janitor moved his broom to sweep it up but Chris grabbed it as if he had not intended to drop the burning cigarette. They bumped heads and Chris said, "Excuse me."

The old man mumbled an apology as he raised his head but then he stared at Chris and his gray eyes widened. "Jed?" he croaked.

Chris thought the man would fall. He put a hand on his shoulder to steady him. "You better sit down. There's a chair at my table."

But the man shook his head. "You put a fright into me," he said. "I thought you were someone I used to know. But you couldn't be. Nigh forty years have passed since I saw him and you haven't seen twenty yet."

Chris wasn't satisfied. "You called him Jed," he said. "That's part of my name, too. They call me Chris, but my full name is Jedidiah Christian Conover the Third."

The man's sunburned face blanched and his hands shook on the broom and dustpan. He said, "I believe I will sit down. I can take my coffee break." He put a trembling hand on Chris' arm and let him lead him to the table.

"I'll get it for you," Chris said. "What do you want?"

"Black coffee. Tell them it's for Charlie Scott. I get it free."

Chris set the cup on the table, turned his own chair around and straddled it. Charlie took a sip of the scalding coffee, swallowed it and smacked his lips. "Just the way I like it," he said, never taking his gaze from Chris' face. "I knew some Conovers back in Texas when I was a young man. You must be Jed's grandson. You're the spitting image of him."

"I guess I do look like him at the same age. I've seen pictures. Aunt Essie has one taken of her and him. I never saw him. He died long before I was born."

"Jed's dead?" Charlie said in such a way that Chris thought he didn't expect an answer. Charlie shook his head as if in a daze. He sat for several minutes while Chris waited in silence. Then he took a swallow of coffee and spat it on the ground. "Cold."

"I'll get you another cup," Jed offered.

"No, I don't have long before I have to get back to work. Tell me about the rest—your aunts and uncles and grandparents. I knew them pretty well back then."

Chris tried to think back to the generation Charlie remembered. He had never paid much attention to the old folks and had little interest in the ones that had died before he could remember. But he liked the old codger and, besides, it felt good to find somebody to talk to about the homefolks he missed so much.

"If you knew them in Texas, then I guess you'd just be interested in my Conover side. How long has it been since you saw any of them?"

Charlie hesitated before he said in a rough voice, "Before they left for Indian Territory. I heard of them once or twice. I heard about Paul getting shot. Did they ever find out who did it?"

Chris shook his head. "I don't know," he said. "It all happened so long ago I haven't heard much talk about it. Let's see. You knew my great grandparents and great aunts and uncles. Nearly all of them stayed in Carter County but Aunt Ida. She's out here in California somewhere. Uncle Plez and Aunt Flora still live on his Indian allotment. Uncle Ben still farms his section of land even though he struck it rich when they found oil on it. Uncle Holt and Aunt Betsy and their families live in Healdton. Grandma Lillie lives next door to Aunt Betsy so she can look after her."

Charlie's face blanched again. He rubbed his gnarled hand over it and seemed lost in deep thought. When he spoke, his voice shook. "I reckon I can trust you, Boy," he said. "I go by Charlie Scott, but it's not my real name. Can I trust you not to reveal my secret?"

For some reason, Chris agreed. He may be a fugitive from the law or some-thing, he thought, but I'm dying to know who he is.

"My real name is Buford Conover. I'm your Grandpa's older brother."

Excitement leaped in Chris like a jackrabbit. He had listened to stories about Great Uncle Buford all his life. Nobody had heard a word from him since he left the country. Chris tried to recall the hazy story; he knew Uncle Buford skipped out to evade arrest or maybe getting killed himself. And here he had bumped into him *accidentally*. Everyone thought he must be dead or some word of him would have found its way back to them.

But Charlie or Buford, whatever his name, kept asking him questions. "Before I left, I heard that the Sexton brothers killed my brother. Do you know anything about that?"

"I don't know anything about them murdering anybody, but I have heard what happened to them. My grandpa was there and saw it all. It happened when my Daddy was a baby but he heard the story many times and he passed it on to me. Al Sexton tried to escape when he worked on a road gang with Grandpa and the guard shot him dead. Daddy said the other brother—I forget his name—finished out his term and left the country. Nobody ever heard from him again."

Buford breathed deeply a few times as if absorbing this news. But when he started talking again, he said no more about it. Instead, he said, "You say my Ma is still alive. What about Pa?"

"He died in the twenties before I was born. I never did meet him or my Grandpa Jed, either. He died in the flu epidemic in 1918."

"I can't believe Jed has a grandson old as you. When did he and Esther get married?"

Puzzled, Chris said, "Aunt Esther is Uncle Ben's wife. You mean," he stopped to think how to put this. "You mean you expected her to marry Grandpa?"

Charlie shook his head in disbelief. "Boy, you never can tell how things will turn out. When I left Ben hadn't even met Esther. And I always checked to be sure that nothing had been set afire when Jed and Esther got together. Yeah, I sure thought they would get married. Who did Jed marry?"

"My Grandma's maiden name was Vinnie Wade. Did you know her?"

Chris couldn't read the expression on Charlie's face when he said, "I've heard of the Wades but I didn't know her. When did they get married?"

"I don't know but my Daddy's thirty-seven this year. He's nineteen years older than I am. I guess it runs in the family to marry young. Do you have any kids?"

"No, no, I never did marry. Tell me more about Ma. I can't believe she is still living. She was always so frail, kind of an invalid. I'd sure like to go see her, but with the war on and everything, I doubt that can happen."

"You can call her. She doesn't have a telephone but she lives right next door to Aunt Betsy. She'll call her to the phone."

"Betsy. Such a little bitsy thing the last time I saw her, I can't get it all through my head. I never thought I'd hear of any of my kin again. I wish I could go right now and see them, but with the wartime restrictions on travel, I'll have to wait. I will call, though. Yes, I'll call as soon as I can. Write down the number for me, will you? And write down how I can stay in touch with you. I'll buy your dinner when I get off work if you'll stick around."

Follow the Conover family from 1908 through 1919 as they and their neighbors experience birth, death, natural disasters, and deprivation as well as good fortune. Their pioneering spirit and hospitality guide them to bury their bitterness and assist others in dire need. As Lillie says, "When people have no place else to go, we have to take them in."

Ben's debts and loss of income force him to postpone his dreams for the future as he becomes the mainstay of his family. His love for Esther sustains him when she agrees to walk out with him even though he realizes she does not feel the same about him.

Jed must live with his hurry-up marriage and try to forget Esther but his love for his children and expression of his artistic abilities make life bearable. Esther tries to put her heartache behind her and make a good life for herself until the night she must face her suppressed feelings for Jed and make decisions that can change her whole life—and Jed's and Ben's.

Family Saga

Oklahoma

Pioneer

Historical

Fiction

Woman Author

Land of Sun and Flowers presents a true-to-life portrayal of family life and need for reliance on neighbors in early Oklahoma.

Author Photo by Danny Williams

Voncille Shipley grew up sitting at the feet of hardy pioneers, absorbing their stories and patterns of speech. Years later she has fulfilled her childhood dream of writing fiction about early times. Encouraged by her husband, John, she presents *Land of Sun and Flowers*, sequel to *This Raw, Red Land*.

0-595-30705-1

This Raw, Red Land - Oklahoma Book Award <u>Finalist</u>
Signed copies of my novels may be ordered directly from me. Please show number of copies of each book on the order form below and mail it with your payment to:

Voncille Shipley
Rt. 1 Box 382
Elmore City OK 73433-9694

Be sure to fill in the <u>Signed to Whom?</u> blank with the name(s) of the recipients exactly the way you want it to appear in the dedication. If you want it mailed to another party as a gift, a gift card will be inserted in the book.

Thank You
(Cut Here)

Name _____

Street _____

City/State_____ Zip _____

Signed to Whom? _____

_____

_____*This Raw, Red Land*— $14.95 ea.—   _____
_____*Land of Sun and Flowers* –$13.95 ea.—   _____
Add $3.00 shipping for each book ordered.   _____
                              Total

Address of Recipient (if different)

_____

_____

Do you want to include a gift card? _____